DISHARMONY OF THE SPHERES

Edited by J Alan Erwine

Disharmony of the Spheres
Edited by J Alan Erwine

First printing October 2017

Nomadic Delirium Press
Aurora, Colorado
http://www.nomadicdeliriumpress.com

For Eryn

Contents

Editor's Introduction
By J Alan Erwine

Mental illness is very common in our society, but it's also very misunderstood. Many view those with mental illnesses as being weak. It's very common for those suffering to hear things like, "Pull yourself together," or "It's going to get better," or, "Stop being such a baby." These aren't the types of things that one would tell someone who is suffering from cancer or diabetes, or some other "physical" illness, but for those with mental illness, it's an all too common occurrence.

I know this because I have seen it so many times. Working in the science fiction and fantasy field, I have seen so many other authors, editors, publishers, and fans that deal with one form of mental illness or another. I'm not sure if the field, being a "fringe field," attracts these types of people, or if it's something else, but got to any convention and you will see many people that are "suffering" from mental illness.

I also know what it's like to deal with mental illness because I have been dealing with chronic depression since adolescence, and I sometimes think that the fact that I've made it to "something" years old is a bit of a miracle, as in my deepest funks, I've often contemplated suicide, as have many others who suffer from this disease…and it is a disease.

For a couple of years I had been toying with the idea of doing an anthology of this sort, and then when one of my daughters went through a serious depression, I committed myself to finishing this anthology…a commitment that is not always easy when dealing with depression, as completing things can be difficult.

When I finally decided to create this anthology, I decided I wasn't going to just do a collection about people suffering from various mental illnesses, I decided that I was going to do an anthology about people overcoming these illnesses, maybe not defeating their illness, but at least showing that people that are mentally ill can be successful.

Those struggling with mental illness should not be viewed as weak, they should be seen as strong, because it takes a great deal of courage to battle through every day when it seems like your own mind is against you

I also decided that I didn't want to just show people being successful, I wanted to help people in the "real" world as well. That's why I decided that half of all of the profits from this book would go to the "Yellow Ribbon Suicide Prevention Program," an organization dedicated to helping prevent teen suicide. To learn more, please go to ww.yellowribbon.org.

I'd like to thank all of the authors that contributed to this collection. The stories blew me away when I read them, and I hope that when others read them, they'll realize that people with mental illness shouldn't be scorned, but rather they should be praised for their successes, and I also hope that if any of the readers are themselves suffering from any form of mental illness that maybe they'll be inspired by one or more of these stories.

In closing, I'd just like to say that if you are suffering from depression, PTSD, anxiety, or any other mental illness, you are not alone, and you can be strong, no matter what the world might try to tell you.

-J Alan Erwine
-October 11, 2017

Time of the Bursting
By Ian Brazee-Cannon

"He's up on the roof, pacing aimlessly and blowing bubbles."

"Blowing bubbles?"

"Yep. Won't talk to anyone."

"We don't have time for these kinds of games right now. I'll go talk to him."

Through the vents, Phillip could hear everything that was being said on the floor below him. He knew everyone thought he was overreacting. There was a job that needed to be done and he should be professional and not let his recent family issues get in the way of doing his job. His life was falling apart, yet his position at the lab made it next to impossible to take time off during this crucial period.

The moment he entered the building his whole body had gone numb. The idea of trying to interact with other members of the team left him overwhelmed with anxiety. Pleasantries were exchanged as Phillip passed by, but he said little to any of them. His responses were nothing more than reflex replies. The world around him was all just a blur. The quicker he found a corner to vanish into, the better. He still had no idea what had been going through his mind at the time, but he grabbed a bottle of soap bubbles off a desk and made his way to the roof without a word to anyone.

That was over an hour ago. At least a dozen team members had tried to talk to him, but it was as if there were some manner of barrier around him. No one seemed to want to get very close to him.

"Okay Phillip, I know you're going through a lot right now, but this is not the day to lose focus."

Phillip stopped pacing. He drew the plastic wand to his lips and blew. The train of bubbles flowed over his head to quickly vanish from his sight.

"Give me a moment more," Phillip said.

"Be in the lab in five minutes."

Phillip stood motionless until he heard the door fully close. After blowing another group of bubbles, he made his way to the edge and looked out at the world. He was five stories up. In the past, he would have felt a slight sense of vertigo, yet now he stood there, unmoving, without a trace of unease. None of it felt real. The browning grass covered hills. The harsh concrete parking lot filled with colorful transports of all makes. The 'V' of birds that flew below the patchwork of thinning clouds. It was all familiar, yet out of place and wrong.

"One small step and I'd be free of the pain..."

Phillip took in a deep breath and let loose one last round of bubbles before turning to the stairs and taking his leave of the roof.

*

Excitement flowed from the lab as Phillip entered. He produced his best smile and hoped it looked real enough. This was a big day for the group, even if it all felt meaningless to Phillip. The series of pats on his back were felt without any awareness of who gave them.

"Doctor Tennant, good to see you," the young lab tech at the controls said. "All readings look promising. They've been triple checked already. If you'd like to look them over before we proceed?"

Phillip closed his eyes and took in a deep breath. He opened his eyes and, with forced focus, looked towards the collection of monitors in front of him. The oxygen levels looked fine while the nitrogen levels were on the low side, but within acceptable range. He reached over and adjusted the nitrogen input slightly. The radiation levels were all showing to be firmly in the safe zones.

"Keep an eye on those nitrogen levels. We don't want them dropping too low."

"Yes sir."

"Any sign of movement in the chamber?"

"No sir."

The stats on the health monitors all were satisfactory.

Phillip looked up into the chambers beyond the glass. The soft blue glow of the artificial swamp, as identical as possible to the birthing swamplands of Vina, had a haunting feel to it. Dozens of soft pale orange pods floated in the nutrient rich water, which was a thick blueish sludge.

Looking at what would be the first Vanivians to ever be bursted (the scientifically accepted best term to describe how the Vanivians started life) off of their homeworld, Phillip remembered he had once

14

felt true excitement when looking at all they had achieved here. It now felt pointless to him. He was just going through the motions in order to keep everyone around him comforted.

"How many membranes have gone optimal?"

"We are at 87 percent, as of last inspection."

"All is as it should be then. If this is going to happen, today is the best chance of it. Although it could be a long day of waiting if..."

The crowd fell silent with the slight movement from within the chamber.

"Was that a pod?"

"Yes sir," the lab tech replied, a huge smile on his face.

All eyes were now drawn to the artificial swamp. One of the pods was now shifting and bulging as if it were awakening. The movement of the one pod started a chain reaction as other pods nearby seemed to be awakened by the movement. It short order over half the pods were showing signs of life.

"I read the descriptions, but it really is amazing to see it first hand," the lab tech commented.

"Yeah," Phillip replied. "Johnson, suit up and get in there."

Not five minutes later the team member was wading through the artificial swamp in a suit that would look more fitting on a fisherman in the middle of a stream than on a decorated scientist at one of the most advanced labs in the galaxy. A pair of dark rubber waders raised up to his chest, which was covered by a green wet suit. A foam saucer covered with various tools, floated behind him, attached to his belt by a three foot long cord. A transparent face mask hung down from his forehead. On his hands were what looked to be white mountain climbing gloves covered with blue rubber bumps.

"This is Doctor Jonas Johnson on day 277 of the Vanivian Transplant Project," Doctor Johnson stated loudly, knowing all he did and said was being recorded. "Yesterday the majority of Vanivian pods displayed the characteristics of the final stages leading up to bursting. As of 09:42 today we witnessed the prerequisite activity signaling readiness for bursting. I have suited up and have entered the artificial environment. I am now approaching the center of the pod grouping."

The documentation registered as nothing more than noise to

Phillip. He stood still, his gaze was towards the activity in the artificial swamp. While he looked to be focused on the events taking place there, all he saw was a smudge on the far wall.

As Doctor Johnson continued the narration of his activity, he raised a wiggling pod out of the sludge and gripped it tightly. He moved in to get a better look at the lifeform inside.

"I am holding a highly active pod," Johnson stated. "The Vanivian inside looks to be healthy and is clearly clawing at the membrane. There are several other pods that look to be at the same stage. I would say the first burstings are just minutes away."

A muffled splat came from just behind Johnson.

"Sounds like the first one has burst. Oh, and they were not kidding about the smell."

Dr. Johnson faced the origin of the sound and a moment later turned back, holding a small pale green, slimy creature. The body was a bulb with four identical looking limbs swirling about uselessly in the air. A head as large as the body awkwardly hung there with a large mouth opening wide. A unique blueish streak ran down the left side of its body.

"Our first burster looks healthy. Designation is Alpha." Johnson held the creature up to a camera mounted on the wall and moved it around to ensure full documentation. "Going to place Alpha in the nursery pool." Dr. Johnson turned and lowered his hand into a calm pool of swamp water that was separated from the water with the pods by an artificial plant wall. As soon as Alpha found itself in the water its legs took control and it was moving with graceful ease. Its head stayed beneath the water with the mouth wide open. A small blowhole on its belly stayed above the water and pulled in air.

As the crowd watched the newly bursted swimmer going at it, a series of splats came from the pod pool.

Dr. Johnson stood still, a look of disgust on his face. A splatter of pale green/gray slime had made it past his faceguard.

"I'm going to let someone else have this honor next time," Johnson joked as he continued the documentation process with the newly bursted Vanivians.

Phillip did his job and stayed at his position for a little while longer. After the fourteenth burst, when all looked to be going smoothly, he was able to justify taking his leave.

"Keep those nitrogen levels stable," Phillip said as he turned from the monitors.

"Yeah, got it," the lab tech casually replied.

He passed through the barrage of congratulations and back pats fully detached from the moment. He made his way to the staff overnight rooms, found one that was unclaimed and crawled into the simple fold away bed there.

There was no sleep for Phillip. He lay there with his eyes closed, his mind lost in thoughts he wished he could escape from. He knew that much of what was going through his mind was irrational. That didn't lessen the impact of it all. The unreasonable concepts merged with the rational concerns, feeling equally valid. No matter how hard he tried, there was no escape from his own mind. Once more he found his thoughts going to dark places as he wondered how he could keep living with the pain, or if it was even worth it to try.

He let himself drift away in a half-awake state, removed from the world.

Time must have past.

"Doctor Tennant," came the frantic voice from somewhere in the darkness. "They need you in the lab now. There have been complications."

Phillip opened his eyes and looked at the young woman standing in the doorway. She was an intern. He knew her name, but it was not coming to him.

He dragged himself out of bed and followed her back to the lab without saying a word. She was clearly excited about something.

In the lab, just outside the artificial environment, the crowd has been cleared an only essential personal were there. The eight team members were clearly agitated. Dr. Johnson was once more suited up and in the murky waters as the other scientists looked over the equipment, loudly stating the readings and their meanings.

"Dammit Phillip, where have you been? This is not the time to be hiding and wallowing in self-pity. In the last two hours we have gone from having 68 viable swimmers to only 11, and those are not looking healthy. Pull yourself together and do your job."

Phillip stared at his teammate. He had heard all the words, but it took him some time to process just what had been said. He understood what was at stake, but none of it seemed important to him.

Phillip walked over and took a look at the monitors. Once more he noted the nitrogen levels had fallen again. Once more it was on the lower side of the acceptable range, but not optimal.

"Let me try something," Phillip said as he moved back and left the room.

"What's he doing?"

"Let him be. If he can't focus, he's no use to us right now."

Phillip pulled on a pair of waders and grabbed a tank of nitrogen with a connecting hose attached before entering the artificial swamp. He made his way into the nursery pool. He said nothing as he motioned for Dr. Johnson to move aside. In the water the 11 Vanivian swimmers floated, barely moving. Their skin had turned dull gray and was stretched tight around their bodies.

He twisted the nob on the cylinder. He held the end of the hose up to the frontal blowhole of the closest swimmer. The little creature took in a large breath. Its limbs raised up, attempting to grab at the hose.

In no time at all, the swimmer's skin regained its green color and loosened up as the little guy became active again.

"Raise the nitrogen levels," Phillip stated. He handed the nitrogen cylinder off to Dr. Johnson, who didn't need to be told what to do.

Phillip stumbled back until he found himself up against the wall. He adjusted his weight and was able to sit back against the wall. He looked up at saw the Vanivian swimmer had followed him. It swam up to him. He removed one of the rubber gloves and reached down and rubbed the back of his hand against the moist skin of the swimmer. The little guy clasped itself to Phillip's hand.

Phillip raised his hand and held it out in front of his face. He looked at the minuscule creature clinging to him. A distinctive blueish streak ran down the left side of its body.

"Hello Alpha," Phillip said.

In the examination of the fragile alien creature a cloud seemed to lift from Phillip's mind. This slimy little being made sense to him and felt right. He raised his other hand and gently petted Alpha.

His face felt wet. It took him a moment to realize he had been crying.

Phillip smiled.

Phoenix

By Sharon Lee and Steve Miller

Cyra hurried through the bustle of the pre-dawn, head down, and face hidden.

She traveled early, when the friendly shadows helped hide her deformity, allowing her to negotiate the eight chancy blocks from the anonymous apartments she kept in a nondescript building--where the floor numbering was in fresher paint in Terran numerals than in the older Liaden--to the streets she depended upon for her living.

Once on those streets no one remarked her, and few noticed her passing or her business, except those who had need to buy or sell this or that bauble of stone or made-stone or metal. The half-light suited her purpose, and even so, she sometimes found herself automatically facing away from the odd passerby of Liaden gait and stature who would consider her worthless, or less.

On some worlds, Cyra would have been valued for her intelligence and her skills. On others, her demeanor and comeliness would surely have been remarked.

On others--but none of that mattered, for here on Liad she was marked for life by the knife of her Delm, and guaranteed a painful existence without the support of clan or kin for at least the remaining ten years of the dozen she'd been banned from clanhouse and the comforts of full-named society.

At one time, of course, she'd been Cyra chel'Vona, Clan Nosko. Now, on the streets where she was seen most, she was "that Cyra," if she was anything at all.

The marks high on her cheeks were distinctive, but hardly so disfiguring or repulsive in themselves to have people of good standing turn their heads or their backs on her until she passed. Yet, those of breeding did....

This was scarcely a problem any longer, for she had long ago moved the shambles of her business from the streets of North Solcintra, where she had served the Fifty, to the netherworlds of Low Port, where her clientele were most frequently off-worlders, the clanless, outlaws, and the desperate.

Her own fortunes had fallen so far that she opened and closed her small shop by herself, working daily from east-glow to mid-day, and then again from the third hour until whatever time whimsey-driven traffic in the night faltered. Occasionally even these hours were insufficient to feed her, and she would work in the back-house at Ortega's--cleaning dishes, turning sheets, cooking, pushing unruly drunks out the back door--where her face would not be remarked--and thereby eating and sometimes earning an extra bit or two.

That was the final indignity. Very often her purse was so shrunken that she measured her worth not in cantra or twelfths but in bits--Terran bits!--and was pleased to have them. For that matter, being employed by a pure blood Terran was, by itself, enough to turn any of the polite society from her face, no matter that the Terran was a legal land-holder.

Things had been somewhat better of late; the new run of building on the east side of the port gave many of her regulars a chance at day labor and those of sentimental bent often returned in hope for the items they'd sold last week, or even last year.

This morning she was tired, having spent much of the evening at Ortega's, filling in for a cook gone missing. Shrugging her way into the store after touching the antiquated keypads, she caught a glimpse of someone standing huddled against the corner of the used clothing store.

Closing the door behind her, leaving behind the sound of the morning shuttles lifting under the clouds, and the jitneys in the streets, she settled into the quiet of the thick-walled old building, checking the time to see that she was early enough to set tea to boil, and to warm and wolf the leftover rolls she carried from last night's work. She started those tasks, glancing through the scratched flex-glass of the door as she moved the few semi-valuable pieces from their hiding places to the case, and uncovered the special twirling display that held her choice Festival masks behind a clear plastic shield.

Cyra admired the green feathered mask as it twirled by, recalled the evening her aunt had brought her the ancient box and said, "This green does not become me, and I doubt I'll go again to Festival. This was *my* aunt's, after all, and is much out of style--but if you wish it, it is yours."

And so she'd worn it to her first Festival, finding delight in the games of walking and eyeing, the while looking for people she might know and seeking one who might not know her....

Later, she'd been doubly glad of that Festival, for the marriage her uncle found for her was without joy *or* success, which had scandalized him despite the medic's assurance that she was healthy--and quashing her chance at full time study at the Art Institute.

Now, of course, she was denied the Festival at all.

She took her hand from beneath the plastic shield, where it had strayed, unbidden, and returned to routine, eyes drawn to the sudden flash of color outside the window, as the light began to rise with real daybreak.

He--at the distance the wildly abundant Terran beard was about all she could be sure of, aside from the bright blue skullcap he wore to hide his hair--*he* was dressed in what may have once been fine clothes, but which looked somewhat worse than they ought. She doubted he could see her, but his face and eyes seemed to spend about half their time watching her shop door and the other half watching chel'Venga's Pawnshop.

She sighed gently. The ones who had not the good sense to wait until the store was respectably open were the ones who were selling something. She wasn't sure which sort was worse--the ones who needed something they wouldn't be able to afford or the ones who couldn't afford to sell what they had to offer for a price she was able to give. At least he'd be out soon, no doubt, and she'd be able to keep the fantasy she held to heart from being overly tarnished yet again, the fantasy that Port Gem Exchange was yet a jewelry store and not yet a pawnshop in truth.

The clock stared back at her. Once upon a time she had slept until mid-day when she wished. Now she used each hour as if there was not a moment to waste. And for what this early morning? So that she might eat without being observed, and without companions. No need to rush--chel'Venga's Pawnshop rarely opened on time.

*

The Terran stood at his corner across the way, left hand in pocket, watching across the way as the increasing jitney traffic blocked his view from time to time, his beard waving in the wind. He'd seen her work the door and had straightened; and was there when she went back inside to get the rope-web doormat that welcomed her visitors. The pawnshop had no such amenities as rugs or mats. Perhaps it made no difference to her customers, but such were among the few luxuries she had these days.

He was not on the corner when she straightened from placing the mat in doorway and a quick glance showed him nowhere on the street. The lights had gone on in the pawnshop. They'd likely stolen the man away. Now Cyra regretted not giving in to the impulse to beckon to him as she unlocked the door, no matter the poor manners of it. It was hard to keep good melant'i in this part of the city, after all.

And then he was back, this time carrying a large, flat blue package of some kind, and he was hurrying, fighting the wind and the traffic, threatening at one point to run into a jitney rather than risk his burden.

Then he was there, larger than she'd realized, his relative slenderness accentuating his height, the dense beard distorting and lengthening his already long face, and his plentiful dark brown hair, brushed straight back from the high forehead, making him seem that much taller now that he'd taken the hat respectfully off to enter her store.

He came in quietly, with the noise of a large transport lifting from the port masking not only his sounds but those of the door until it closed, leaving his breathing--and hers--loud in the room.

He glanced down at her, nodded Terran-style, and looked over the shop carefully. Somehow, she felt he might be looking at the tops of the cases--it had been many days since she'd thought to dust them, for who ever climbs a stool to inspect them?

He smiled at her, his light brown eyes inspecting her face so quickly that she hadn't time to flinch at the unexpected attention; nodded again, and said in surprisingly mannered Liaden, "I regret it has taken me so long to find your operation. I suspect we are both the poorer for it. "

At that he pulled from his pocket a large handful of glittery objects, some jeweled, some enameled or overlaid; pins, rings, earrings, necklaces....

And, she suspected quickly, all of them real.

"These are for sale," he said, "for a reasonable return. Since I am very close to crashing I will not haggle nor argue. I will simply accept or reject your offers on each. I would hope to get more than scrap value. You are a jeweler, however, and will know what you need."

His hands were the competent hands of an artisan, she decided as he turned the items out on her sales cloth. Despite the items he sold, he was ringless and despite the worn look of his clothes the marks on his hands were those of someone who worked with them regularly, not one who was careless or unemployed. Indeed, there were spatters, or patterns of colors on his skin, masked somewhat by the unusual amount of hair on his wrists, on the back of his hands, even down to his knuckles. Cyra was distracted, yes, even shocked: she had never seen a man with hair so thick it looked like fur!

"Indeed, we shall look," she managed, fretting at herself for the incivility of staring at someone's hands.

Quickly she sorted, finding far too many items of real interest. A dozen earrings--some of them paired and some not--all of quality. A strangely designed clasp pin, set with diamonds, starstones, and enamel work. A necklace, of platinum she thought, set with amethyst. Then the glass was in her hand, and the densitometer turned on, and the UV light, as well.

In a twelve day she would rarely expect to see so many fine pieces, much less at once.

"The pin," she said finally, "is obviously custom work. I suspect it of more value to the owner or designer than to me...."

"My great-uncle designed that himself," said the man, "and he is always one for the gaudy. Set it aside and we can talk about it later. Else?"

Cyra looked up--way up--into those brown eyes. He looked at her without sign of distress, and so she continued, oddly comforted.

"I would offer to buy the lot if we were closer to Festival," she admitted, "even the pin. But these are all quality items, as you do know, and they are somewhat more--extravagant, let us say--than I might usually invest in at this season."

"That's not an offer," the Terran returned, his face suddenly strained. "And I will need something for later, too."

"Perhaps," she suggested, "you should choose those least dear to you and point them out to me. I will offer on them."

His hands carefully moved the earrings to a small pile, and the necklace, leaving the pin by itself, and retrieving deftly other pins and the two rings. He leaned his hands on the counter then, as if tired.

"An offer," he said, "with and without the pin. You know that it is platinum; know that it is platinum from the very Amity object--and the provenance can be proved...."

Cyra grabbed up the pin, admiring its weight and the clasp design. Impulsively she touched his hand, the one that held the other retrieved objects, and turning it over, pressed the pin into it.

"In that case, this is better placed with someone among the High Houses. They fail to arrive here in sufficient number to make my purchase worthwhile...."

And then she named a price which was far more of her available capital than she normally risked--but far less than the value she perceived before her--and was oddly annoyed by the man's rather curt, "That will do."

She was even more annoyed by the rapt attention he paid as she counted the cash out--as if each coin was in doubt. The she realized he was looking at her face. Involuntarily, she colored, which made her angry. Too long among the Terrans if she could blush so easily....

"No," he said suddenly, his Liaden gone stiffly formal. " I did not mean to disturb you. I sought--I was trying to see if I might read or recognize the etchings or tattoos on your face."

Cyra felt her face heat even more. She covered the scars with close-held fingers, looking up.

"Our transaction is finished. You may go."

He reached his hand toward her face and she flinched.

"Ah," he said, wisely. "The rule is that you may reach and touch my hand, but I, I may not reach and touch yours. When the crash is coming I see things so clearly...."

Startled, she stepped back.

"Forgive me," she managed, and paused, seeking the proper words. Indeed, *she* had overstepped before he had; it was folly to assume that one who was Terran had no measure of manners.

Then: "But why this crash? Crash? You do not seem to be on drugs or drink, and..."

Now she was truly flustered; more so when he laughed gently.

"In truth, I am very much on drugs right now. I have been drinking coffee constantly for the last three days. Starting last night, I have been drinking strong tea, as well. It has almost been enough, you see, but I could tell it would not continue to work, so I need to buy food--I should eat very soon--I need to write the notes, though, and look once more before the crash."

Cyra held her hands even closer to her face.

"You need not look at all. These are none--"

But he was shaking his head, Terran-wise.

"No, you misunderstand. I need to look at the art so I remember what comes next... sometimes it is not so obvious to me when I start moving again."

Cyra was sure she *must* be misunderstanding--but before she could reply he pocketed the coins from the counter top and hefted the fabric-covered blue case or portfolio he'd brought in, laying it across the counter and reaching quickly for the seals.

"You, you love beautiful things--you must see this!" he said, nearly running over his words in his haste. "This one is my best so far! This is the reason I have come to Liad....this is where the Scouts are!"

Now he wasn't staring at Cyra at all, and she found the willpower to bring her hands down and come forward to see what might be revealed.

Some kind of tissue was swirled back from inside the case and before her was a photograph of a double star--with one redder and the other bluer--taken from the surface of an obviously wind-swept desert world with tendrils of high gray clouds just entering the photograph.

But sections were missing or else the photo-download had been incomplete or--

Now the odor came to her, eerily taking her back to the brief time she studied painting before turning to jewelry.

"You painted this? You are painting it now?" She looked up into his face and rapidly down to the work again. The detail was amazing, the composition near perfect, the--

"Yes," he was saying, "yes, it is my work. But I must not paint *now*, because now I am tired and spent and will only ruin what I have done. For now, the work is not safe near me!"

Cyra recalled working long and hard on her first real commission, so long and hard in fact that she'd finally fallen asleep in the midst, and woke to find the beaten metal scratched and chewed in the polishing machine, destroyed by the very process which should have perfected it.

She heard her voice before she realized she was speaking--

"If you need a place--I can keep it here. It will be safe! Then, when you are awake and ready, you can claim it."

He laughed, sudden and short, and with an odd twist of amusement pulling his grin into his beard.

"When I wake. Yes, that is a good way to put it. When I wake."

With a flourish he waved his hand over the tissue, swept it back over the painting, and sealed the portfolio.

"My name," he said quite formally, "is Harold Geneset Hsu Belansium. Among my family I am known as Little Gene. To the census people I am BelansiumHGH, 4113." He paused, smoothed his beard, and smiled wryly before continuing.

"When I'm lucky, the pretty ladies of the universe call me Bell. Please, lady, if I may have your name, I would appreciate it if you would call me Bell."

With that he handed the portfolio into her care.

She bowed. "Bell you wish? Then Bell it is. I am Cyra the Jeweler to the neighbors here, or simply Cyra. I will see you when you wake."

*

Sound rumbled through the walls and rattled the room around Cyra, who involuntarily looked toward the ceiling. This one was an explosion then--more blasting, for the expansion-- and not a re-routed transport flying low overhead. Rumor had it that several of the older houses two streets over were settling dangerously, but that was just rumor as far as she was concerned. Her store would be fine. It *would*.

She tried to tell herself it was just the noise that was making her skittish, but she knew it wasn't so. She had moved the stool behind the counter to gain a better vantage of the street, and had developed a nervous motion--nearly a shake of the head it was--when surveying the street.

The knowledge that she had a masterwork of art in her back room awaiting the return of the absent Bell frightened her deeply.

Suppose he didn't return? Suppose he had "crashed" in some fey Terran way and was now locked in a quiet back room at Healers Hall, or worse?

A smartly dressed businessman carrying a bag from the pastry shop strode by and Cyra found herself looking anxiously past him toward the corner where she'd first spotted Bell. It didn't help--the businessman had slowed, eyes caught by one of her displays, perhaps--and now was peering in and reaching for the door, carefully wiping feet, and bringing the brusque roar of a transport in with him as he entered. He closed the door and the sound faded.

Cyra slid to her feet.

"Gentle sir." She bowed a shopkeeper's bow. "How may I assist you today?"

He bowed, and now that she did not have the advantage of the stool, she saw that he was very tall, with sideburns somewhat longer than fashionable and--no, it was a very thin Terran-style beard, neatly trimmed and barely covering chin.

"Cyra, I am here to bring you a snack and to collect my painting."

She gawked, matching the height, and the color of the beard, and the voice--

"Bell!"

He laughed, and said mysteriously "You, too?"

"Forgive me," she said after a moment. "You gave me great pause. I have been watching for you--but I did not..."

He put the bag on the counter and began rooting through it, glancing at her as if calculating her incomplete sentence to the centimeter.

"I clean up well, eh? But here--if you'll make some tea the lady at the pastry shop assures me you're partial to these..."

"Pastry shop? What does that have to do with anything?" She sputtered a moment, and-- "Eleven days!" She got out finally, which was both more and less than she wished to say.

He lived very much in his face, the way Terrans do; his eyes were bright and his smile reached from the corners all the way to his bearded chin. He laughed gently, patting the counter, where there were now half-a-dozen pastries for her to choose from.

"Yes," he acknowledged. "Eleven. Not too bad. The worst was twenty-four, but that was before I knew enough to keep food by, and I'd been partying instead of painting."

"But what did you do for eleven days?"

He shook his head and the grin dissolved. He glanced down, then looked back to her, eyes and face serious.

"I crashed. I slept and I tried to sleep. I spent hours counting my failures, numbering my stupidities. I counted transports and the explosions and watched the crack in the wall get larger with each. Every so often I knew I'd never see my painting again, and I would know that I'd been taken and that you'd fled the city and I would never see you again, either."

He raised his hand before she could protest. "And then I would pull myself together and say 'Fool! Bewitched by beauty again!' And that way I'd recall your face and the painting, and try to sleep, knowing you'd be here, if only I could recall the shop name when I walked by. I nearly didn't, you know. I had to focus on that set of ear cuffs that match yours before I was sure."

She nearly reached for her ear, and then she laughed, somehow.

"Forgive me. I am without experience in this *crashing* you do. I was concerned for you, for your health, for your art!"

He smiled slowly. "We're both concerned for my health then, which I'm sure will be greatly improved if I can eat. My stomach has been growling louder than the shuttles! Please, join me! Afterward I will need to visit the port--it would be good if you could do me the favor of retaining my art until I return." The smile broadened. "I promise--I will not be gone eleven days, this time."

The noise of the street invaded their moment then, as two young and giggling girls entered. They stopped short, staring at the towering, bearded figure before them.

"Please," said Cyra to Bell. "If you will come back here we can let my patrons look about!"

He nodded, and moved without hesitation.

She opened the counter tray to let him pass, indicated a low stool for him (his knees seemed almost to touch his ears!) and moved the pastries to the work table, where they would both be able to reach them.

He smiled at her as she lifted a pastry to her lips. She felt almost giddy, as if she'd discovered some new gemstone or precious metal.

*

Debbie, the half-Terran pastry maker from the shop four doors down was in, again, when Cyra returned from apartment hunting. It didn't improve her mood much; the girl hardly seemed as interested in the goods as in Bell, and her language was sprinkled with Terran phrases Cyra could just about decipher on the fly. Likewise, the assistant office manager from the Port Transient Shelter. Didn't they realize that--she shushed her inner voice, nodding, Terran fashion, to Bell in his official spot behind the trade counter. He winked at her and she sighed. Were Terrans always so blatant?

The conversation continued unabated: and there on the counter were actual goods; an item she didn't recognize, so it was for sale to the shop.

"Now," Bell was saying carefully, "I've seen places that these might have been in the absolute top echelon."

The women gazed at him.

Drawn to the story and the voice despite the crowd, Cyra leaned in to hear.

"Of course, that would only be if the local priestess had purified the stone before it was cut, blessed the ore the silver had come from, sanctified the day the day the ring was assembled, and then prayed over the ring-giver and scried the proper hour for giving."

"In other corners of the universe," he went on, "as, say, on Liad or Terra, the flaws in the stone might mark it ordinary. If I were you, I would ask Cyra if she'll set a price, knowing it for a nubiath'a hastily given..."

Cyra moved behind the counter to take up the office of buyer, but the women had both apparently heard tall tales from Terrans in the past--

"Bell, now really, were you on that planet," asked the assistant office manager, "--or have you merely heard of it?"

He rolled his eyes and surprised Cyra with a discreet pat as she squeezed by him.

"What, am I a spaceman, or a Scout, to have all my stories disbelieved?"

They laughed, but he continued, assuming a serious air.

"Actually, it was almost all a disaster. The planet you should never go to is Djymbolay. I arrived just after I finished a painting on board the liner, and was pretty well spent. I had my luggage searched twice for contraband, and then they confiscated the painting as an unauthorized and unsanctified depiction of the world."

He shook his head, then tapped it with his finger. "They wanted to have me put away for blasphemy or something, I think. It took a Scout who happened by--all thanks to little John!--to let me keep my papers and my paint and my freedom. Off with my head or worse, I expect was the plan! But the Scout was there on another matter and interceded. The locals walked me across the port under armed guard, and the Scout came, too, to be sure that it was gently done--and they kept me confined to the spaceport exit-lounge for the twelve days the ship was there. If several kind ladies hadn't taken pity, and brought me meals and blankets, I might well have starved and froze."

Cyra bit back a comment half-way to her lips; after all she knew not where he'd slept before she met him, nor, for that matter, that he always returned to his own rooms on the afternoons and evenings he went to the lectures at Scout Academy. She only knew he returned to the store with sketches and ideas and full of hope that he might eventually be permitted to visit a new world, to be the first painter, the first interpreter....

In a few moments more, the transaction was made; she paid a fairly low price for the emerald ring--the one suggested by the seller--and agreed to look at earrings that might be a match.

The two women gone. Bell looked at her carefully.

"You're tired--and you've been angry."

Exasperated by his grasp of the obvious, Cyra waved her hands in the air in a wild gesture, and snapped, "How else?"

"You might be pleased, after all. The emeralds were got at a decent price."

"Yes, a decent price. But if I'm going to afford you, my friend, we'll need to do better."

He looked at her with the same air of frankness he'd used when talking about the disaster that had cost him a painting, and shook his head.

"Yes, I know; I am hardly convenient for myself, much less for anyone else."

"That's not what I meant!" she protested. "I mean that--I mean that it is difficult to find a larger place to live hereabouts, and nearer to my apartment there are those who will not rent to someone who--"

"Someone who might bring a Terran home of a night," Bell finished, as she faltered. "Inconvenient I said, and I meant! " he insisted with heat. "I don't mind sleeping here in the store, after all, though the light is not always good. Perhaps you can offer to rent the corner place the next street over."

They had been over that before, too. Bell's situation was so changeable that neither knew how long they might find each other's company pleasant, useful, or convenient. He could hardly sign a lease, with his "transient alien" status in the port computers assuring that any who looked would laugh at his request. Even getting a room beyond the spaceport was difficult for him, except here in the Low Port area. Mid-port was too dear for his budget in any case.

He could hardly co-sign with her, either. The conditions her Delm had set were strict and might well bear on that--if she wished to ever return to the House, she would, during her time of exile, refrain from forming formal alliances; she must not buy real estate; she was forbidden to marry, or to have children....

There could be no co-signing; she could speak for none other than herself. But to add a place where some of his paintings could be shown--this close to the port, they might gain a better clientele with such a gallery.

Truth told, though, Bell's sometime presence permitted Cyra to cut her dependence on Ortega's chancy employ; in fact, twice recently they'd been there as patrons.

He looked at her, snatched the ring to his hand and began tossing it furiously into the air. This, after three previous ragged forty-day cycles, she recognized. Any day, perhaps any moment, he would drag out the rough sketches and ideas, choose one, and then hardly see her, even should she stand naked before him, while he took plasboard and tegg-paint and the secret odds and ends from his duit box and transformed them by touch of skilled hand and concentration and willpower unmatched to art as fine as ever she'd seen. Days, he would be one with the art.

And then he would crash; folding into a hollow and dispirited being barely willing to feed himself, with a near-fear of sunlight and a monotone voice and no plans to speak of ... until the cycle came full and from the gray, desperate being emerged Bell, fresh and whole and new. Again.

He shook the ring, tossed it, glanced anxiously to his art kit where it was stashed near the door to the back room.

"I know," he said. "I know! It's almost time. I think we should close early, perhaps, and go someplace fine to eat--I'll pay!--and plan on a bottle of good wine and snacks--I've chosen them already--and a night, a glorious night, my beauty. And then, we can talk at breakfast, if the art's not here yet, and if it is, we'll talk in a few days."

In front of her then, the choice--and she knew already she'd take it, or most of it. Had she a clan to call on she would pledge her quartershare-- to make this work, she'd--but what she would do *if* was no matter, now. Her quartershare would go--till the twelfth year, at least--into the account of a dead child, just as her invitations--large and small--would go to her Delm, and be returned with the information that she was in mourning and not permitted.

She recalled the discreet caress a few moments earlier, her blood warming...

Tonight she would forget the she was poor and outcast. Bell would take them somewhere with his stash of cash and they would spend as if he were a visiting ambassador instead of an itinerant artist, and then he would--

"Bell," she said gently, "perhaps we should stay until nearer

closing. My friend. I followed your instructions last time, you know--
there are three prepared boards waiting--and I have already an extra
cannister of spacer's tea and you gave me enough for two tins of Genwin
Kaffe last time, so we have that. That is, if you are certain that you won't
talk to the Healers this time."

He looked at her then and his eyes were hungry; she doubted that
hers were not.

"I'll check the boards, Cyra, and make sure that you have room to
work this time, too."

*

Cyra tasted the salt on her lips, and nearly wept as she relaxed
against him. He was so inexhaustible and inventive a lover, she thought,
that perhaps she should have invited the office manager to help out--
and she laughed at the silliness, and he heard her, Bell with his hands
still willing and eager, and his quirky Terran words dragged out of him
in the midsts.

"Now I'm funny. Oh, woe, oh woe..."

She could see him in the half-light he preferred for lovemaking;
just bright enough that the mirrors on the wall might tell an interesting
tale to a glancing eye. She remembered that he'd brought beeswax
candles, along with wine, flowers, that first evening after his very first
return, when he'd somehow parlayed her concern--

She laughed again, this time finding his hair and beard wooly near
her face, and she gently moved to brush them orderly. He had
something more on his mind though, as her hands came in contact with
his cheek; but she held him a moment and he was willing to be calmed.

Of course, she should not stroke his beard and his cheek; she
should not kiss his nose, nor lay her palm on his face, this Terran who
never knew the taboo of it....

"Let's trade," he said, very gently. "A story for a story, a touch for
a touch."

Then he laid his hand on her cheek, spreading his wide hand so
that his thumb and his forefinger spanned her face.

It was late in the night, very nearly morning; the sounds from the
road were not yet impinging on their lair. His breathing, and hers, and
his touch.

34

"I," he said after a moment. " I cannot go to the Healers, because when someone in my family is cured, we lose the art. My father, my grandfather, my uncle--myself. I tried, there once--"

He paused, brushed her hair away from her eyes, kissed her on her nose, covered the marks on her face as if he would wipe them away. "After that painting was stolen from me I could have been locked up forever there, but for the good luck of a Scout's intercession. So, I thought I should get over the crash. I spoke to a doctor and he seemed to make sense, and they gave me a therapy and drugs and an implant...."

"Here!"

He guided her hand and held it against that long scraggly scar on his leg. She'd found that scar before, but never dared question--there were things lovers were not to ask, after all; the Code was clear on that.

"Three months," he said very quietly. "Let me say about two of my usual cycles, though they change sometimes--be warned!--and I had not even the slightest twinge of being able to paint, and what I drew was stick figures and bad circles and patterns, and I spoke politely to people and one night I went home and picked up a cooking knife and thought that I would cut my throat."

He took her hand and placed it under his beard, where it was just above his throat, and let her feel the pulse of him, and the smaller, more ragged scar.

"I'd made a start, actually, when I realized that what I wanted was not my throat cut, but my art back. And so I took the knife and opened my leg and took the thirty-four months' worth of implant that was left out of me, and I washed it down the drain."

She stared at him, at once fascinated and horrified, not knowing what to say.

"My cousin," he went on, after a moment. "My cousin Darby. He took the cure and has stayed on it. He's married, he goes to work, comes home, goes to work, comes home--and I have the last piece of sculpture he did before the implant. He was brilliant. He made me look like a bumbling student. But it is gone. Five years and he can't draw a face much less model one; he can't see the images in the clouds!"

He brushed his lips over the mark under her left eye, then kissed the one under her right eye.

"You know," he said quietly, "you are beautiful. I have known beautiful ladies, my friend, and you are very beautiful."

The realization hit her--what he would ask, in exchange for this tale from his soul. Very nearly, she panicked, but he caught her mouth with his, and in a few moments, she relaxed against him.

"My friend," she said, "you can be as cruel as you are wonderful. To cut yourself so--the pain! But I am not so brave as you. I took the cuts from my Delm, in punishment--cut with the blade my family keeps from the early days. Then I wept and cried, and was cast from the house..."

"Does this person yet live?" Not in his deepest despair had she heard his voice so cold.

Cyra looked into his face and saw he meant it--that he contemplated Balance or revenge or--

"No, Bell, you cannot. My Delm was doing duty. I was cut to remind me and to warn others."

He said nothing, but kissed her face again, gently, waiting.

"We are not as rich a house as some others, Clan Nosko; and my Delm, my uncle, is not so easy a spender as you or I. As I was youngest of the daughters of the house--and lived at the clan seat, it being close to my shop--it fell my duty sometimes to spend an afternoon and a night, or sometimes two, doing things needful. And so..."

Here she paused a moment, gently massaging Bell's neck under the beard, imagining all too well....

"So it was," she went on very quietly, with the blood pounding in her ears, "that I was briefly in charge of the nursery, the nurse having been given a discharge for cost or cause, I know not. I had put the child Brendar to bed; a likely boy come to the clan through my sister's second marriage. I changed him once, but he was otherwise biddable. I was trying for my Master Jeweler's license, so I was at study with several books. I read, and read more, hearing no fuss. Then my sister came home, and the child was not asleep, but had died sometime in the night."

There was quiet then.

Finally, he kissed her again, each scar, very carefully.

"I'd thought there must be more, but I see the story now, and I am near speechless. The child died of an accident--

"My incompetence and negligence..."

He pressed a finger to her lips so hard it nearly hurt.

"I am a fool, Cyra, my beautiful friend. I thought it was your own anger, or your own desire, that placed those marks on your face; that you had rebelled against the rules of this world and even now wore them as badges. That they were inflicted by your family to humiliate and destroy you never came to mind..."

He brushed the hair out of her face again.

"I will paint your picture one day, I promise. Your face will be known as among the most beautiful of this world. And they will see that they have lost you, for I'll not let them have you back!"

She had no quick answer for this, and then he said, "Here!" and placed her hand again on the long leg scar.

She felt the welt there--he laughed, nibbled on her earlobe, and moved her hand a bit, murmuring, "Now, lady, *here* if you wish to be pleased!"

She did, and she was.

*

Three days later, Cyra was not so very pleased.

To begin, Bell had become inspired sometime in the night of their pillow talk and when she awoke alone in the dawn she found him sketching like a madman on her couch, barely willing to drag himself away from his work long enough to share a breakfast with her.

He packed his sketches and walked with her to the shop, his eyes as elsewhere as his mind. Twice she had to repeat herself while she spoke with him, and then he disappeared into the back room to work as soon as they reached the store.

In the afternoon he had rushed out of the back room, complaining that she'd not told him the time, and stormed out, on his way to a lecture he particularly wanted to see. Worse, he stormed back, having left his sketchbook and wallet, and dashed off with nary a backward glance. When he didn't return by closing--he sometimes went to discussion groups after the lectures--she'd not expected him to come by her apartment, and he didn't, which grated mightily.

In the morning he wandered in very late, hung over and

exhausted, explaining that he'd met a pack of Scouts at the lecture and talked with them until the barkeep announced shift-change at dawn. He was animated, nearly wildly so, explaining that he might "have a line on" the Scout who had helped him at Djymbolay; that his conversations of the evening had revealed that he owed Balance to that Scout; that he might have an idea for yet another painting; and that when he had more money there was a world he'd have to travel to and--

"I have an appointment, Bell," Cyra said abruptly. "Tell me later!"

She rushed out the door, barely confident--and barely caring--that he'd heed the advent of a customer.

Her appointment was with her tongue--had she stayed and heard more she surely would have said hurtful words.

So she walked, nearly oblivious to the sounds of transports--more this day than others since a portion of the port would be closed late in the afternoon for some final tricksy bit of work for the expansion--and found herself several blocks from her usual streets, in a very old section, where the buildings and the people were barely above tumbledown.

Surprisingly, she saw Debbie-the-pastry-girl hurrying from one of the least kept brick-fronts; Number 83 it was, a regrettable four-story affair sporting ungainly large windows and peeling paint. The peaked, slate roof suggested that the building was several hundred Standards old, and it looked like it had no repair since the day it was built.

Heart falling, she reached into her card case, and removed the slip of paper she had from Bell the day he'd agreed to share his direction with her: Number 83 Corner Four Ave, Room 15.

A shuttle's long rumble began then; she could feel the sidewalk atremble as she watched the pastry girl's blue-and-green hair disappear in the distance. Also on the paper was the pad combination, and with the whine of the shuttle rising behind her, and then over, she stood, and for a moment was tempted to enter Number 83 and find Room 15, open the door, and see if--if...

She turned and walked all the way home for lunch, grasping the paper tightly in her fist.

When she got back to the store, calmer, but heartsore, there was Bell's back vaguely visible in the back room. He heard her enter and yelled out over his shoulder "Any luck?"

"No," she said, quietly. "No luck, Bell."

She slept badly alone, and the rumble of the transports, joined with the not entirely foreign sounds of proctor-jitneys blaring horns as they answered a nighttime summons hadn't helped.

And now, on her store step across the road in the dawn light?

Debbie, cuddling Bell's good jacket in her arms.

*

"Bell's ok," the girl said quickly, shaking her absurd hair back from a remarkably grimy face. "He wasn't bleeding all that much and the medic said he'll do. The proctor, now, he'll be OK, too, other'n his pride's pretty well hurt by getting really whomped--I mean *decked* in front of all his buddies. But there's gonna be some fines to pay, I guess, and he's gotta have a place to live and--"

Cyra stood staring, hard put to sort this tumbled message, clinging at last to the simple, "Bell's OK..."

Debbie was looking at her with desperate eyes. "Cyra, you're a lucky girl, you know? But you're gonna have to get someone down to the jail to get him *out*. He's not the kind of guy that'll get along there, and hey--what it'll take is 'a citizen of known melant'i, moral character, and resources.' I sure don't qualify for the resources part, the melant'i I ain't got and I'm not sure if I qualify for the character part...."

Cyra wasn't too sure about the character part either, though the fact that the girl was here with so many of Bell's belongings argued for her. Arrayed on the step was a ship bag with "Belansium" printed on a tag, four or five studies--paintings and sketches of a woman, who Cyra realized must be herself by the detail of the face--nude in different positions, some small odds and ends in boxes, a small paint kit, a picnic box....

"Tell me again," Cyra demanded. "After we get these inside. From the beginning. I'll make tea."

*

Debbie rushed off while the tea was heating and returned with pastries, and a damp towel, which she was using on the dust and grime on her bare arms.

"I was having company over and wasn't much paying attention to other stuff when I heard one of the transports go over. Things started trembling and--well, wasn't at the stage I thought, then the next thing I know there was a big *cherunk* kind of noise and the front wall just fell out into the street. The whole place got shaky and we all got out. Bell come dashing out from his room carrying something big and square and rushing down the steps with it whiles bricks and roof-stuff falling all around.

"We was outside standing and staring--most everyone out by then, when the whole building kind of slanted over backwards and leaned into the alley. My guy, he's pretty smart, he'd grabbed a bottle of wine on the way out, and we all had a sip, and when it looked like there wasn't any more *up* to fall *down* we went in to see what we could save and to make sure no one was inside--and a bunch of snortheads showed up. One grabbed one of them sketches of you and yelled for some of the others--

"That Bell picked up part of a drainpipe and started hitting and bashing at them guys, and then my guy hit one of 'em with the empty bottle, and then the proctors showed up and Bell wasn't letting no one near his stuff. Proctor kind of waved something in his direction and Bell did this neat little dance step and brought his hand out and lifted the proctor right off his feet. Right quick they was all on him...and I had to explain-- see it was my Ma's building, and all-- but they still got Bell for drunk-and-disorderly, striking a proctor, and I don't know what else. And I can't speak for him!"

"Neither can I," Cyra said. admitted, staring down into her tea and trying not to think of Bell at the hottest part of his cycle, locked away from his paints and pens. "Neither can I."

*

"You have arrived," the receptionist told Cyra, "at a bad time. I have no one to spare to listen to your story, as interesting as it must be. The Scouts are not in the habit of interfering with the proctors on matters of Low Port drunk-and-disorderly ..."

Cyra glared. "He was not drunk--not at this time in the cycle. Disorderly--he did strike a proctor, but--" she stopped, suddenly struck by a thought, and came near to the counter again.

"Have you a Scout named Jon?" she asked.

"Only several," a female voice said from close behind her. Cyra spun, face heating. The Scout tipped her head, eyes bright and manic, as the eyes of Scout's so often were. "Would you wish us to know that it is a Scout named Jon whom the proctors discovered to be drunk and disorderly? I don't find that impossible. Why, I myself have been drunk and disorderly in Low Port. It is excellent practice for the dining situations found on several of the outworlds."

"Captain sig'Radia..." the receptionist began, but the Scout waved a hand.

"Peace. Someone has arrived with time to spare for a story about a drunk and disorderly in Low Port." She cocked a whimsical eyebrow in Cyra's direction, looking her full in the face, as if the disfiguring scars were invisible, or non-existent. "The acoustics of this hallway are quite amazing, but allow me to be certain--I did hear you say 'struck a proctor'?"

Cyra admitted it dejectedly. "But it is not the Scout Jon who did this," she continued, feeling an utter fool. "I had merely thought, since my friend--Bell--was known to the Scout..."

"Ah. And something more of your friend--Bell--if you please? For I do not believe, despite our abundance of Jons, that we have any Scouts named Bell."

Cyra bit her lip. "He is a Terran--an artist. Last night, the apartment house he lived in fell down, and--"

"Now I have the fellow!" Captain sig'Radia cried, and grinned with every appearance of delight. "What we heard on the Port is that he knocked down a prepared, on-duty proctor, barehanded. Quite an accomplishment, though I don't expect the proctors think so. No sense of humor, proctors."

"It must be unpleasant," Cyra murmured, "after all, to be knocked down."

"Oh, wonderfully unpleasant," the Scout agreed happily. "Especially with the rest of your team looking on."

"Yes," Cyra bit her lip, wondering how possibly to explain the cycles, and the tragedy of Bell being without his paints *now*. "If you please, Bell--it is very bad..." she stammered to a halt.

"Complicated, eh?" the Scout said sympathetically. "Come, let us be private."

She took Cyra's arm as if they were long friends, and escorted her out of the main room and down a hall.

"Ah, here we are," the Scout said, and put her palm against a door, which opened willingly, utterly silent.

The lights came up as they walked down the room to the table and chairs. Cyra looked about, marveling at the size of the chamber, her eye caught and held by a projection on the front wall--a planetscape, it was, showing a sun and a great-ringed planet in the distance and a close-up portion of bluish-green atmosphere--

Cyra gasped, recognition going through her like a bolt, though she had never seen this painting, but the composition, the eloquence the *work*--it could only be--

"That is Djymbolay, is it not?" She asked the Scout captain, her voice shaking.

The woman looked at her in open wonder. "It is, indeed. How did you know?"

"My friend Bell painted the original of that." She used her chin to point.

The captain looked, face very serious now. "I see. You will then be comforted to know that the original is safe in the World Room." She looked back to Cyra, her smile crooked.

"And your friend Bell is by extrapolations no more nor no less than Jon dea'Cort's glorious madman. Allow me to see if the Scout is within our reach."

*

Summoned, Jon dea'Cort arrived quickly and heard the tale out with a grin almost as wide as Bell's could be, when he stood at the height of his powers. When all was said, he looked to Cyra, and inclined his head.

"Your Bell, he is at what stage in his continuing journey?"

She blinked against the rise of unexpected tears and made herself meet his eyes squarely. "He is painting. Please--"

He held up a hand. "Yes. You were right to come to us." He looked to Captain sig'Radia, who lifted an eyebrow.

"A change of custody, I think," he said to her. "Certainly, they will insist that he be heard, and fined, but he must be got out of the holding tank at once and allowed to paint before drunk-and-disorderly becomes cold murder."

Cyra sat up, horrified. "Bell would not--" A bright glance stopped her.

"Would he not? Perhaps you are correct. But let us not put him to the test, eh?" He grinned suddenly, Scout-manic. "Besides, I want to see what magic flows from his brush this time."

*

They gave her a room, and a meal, and promised to fetch her, when Bell was arrived. She ate and laid down on the bed, meaning to close her eyes for a moment only...

"Cyra?" The voice was quiet, but unfamiliar. "It is I, Jon dea'Cort. Your Bell is safe."

She sat up, blinking, and found the Scout seated on the edge of her bed, face serious.

"Is he well?" she demanded. "Is he--"

He held up a hand. "Would you see him? He is painting."

"Yes!"

"Come then," he said, and he led her out and down the hall to a lift, then down, down, down, perhaps to the very core of the planet, before the doors opened, and there was another hall, which they walked until it intersected another. They turned right. Jon dea'Cort put his hand against a door, which slid, silently, open, and they stepped into a large and well-lit studio.

Bell at the farther end of the room, his easel in the best light and he was working with that focused, feverish look on his face that she had come to know well--and to treasure.

The Scout touched her hand, and tipped his head toward the door. Cyra followed him out.

"Thank you," she said, feeling conflicting desires to sing and weep. "He will crash--sometime. Often, he knows when, but in a strange place, with this interruption--I do not know. Someone--someone should pay attention to him."

"Surely," the Scout said amiably. "And that someone ought to be yourself, if you are able?"

She hesitated for a moment, thinking of the shop in Low Port, and then inclined her head. "I am able."

*

"Cyra?" She looked up from her work, smiling, and found Bell gazing seriously down at her.

Having gained her attention, he went to a knee, and raised his hand to her face. She nestled her cheek into the caress.

"Are you sorry, Cyra? To leave your home, to be rootless, companioned to inconvenient Bell, and in the sphere of Scouts..."

She laughed and turned her face, brushing her lips against his palm, and straightening.

"What is this? You will be painting tomorrow, my friend; do not try to tease me into believing that you are on the down-cycle!"

He smiled at that, and touched a fingertip to her nose before dropping his hand to his knee. "You know me too well. But, truly, Cyra..."

She put the pliers down and reached out, placing her hands on his shoulders and gazing seriously into his eyes.

"I am not sorry, Bell. Did you not say that you would take me away? You have done so, and I am not sorry at all."

He had kept the other part of that pillow-sworn vow, as well, and the portrait of herself that he had completed in Scout Headquarters remained there, on display in the reception area, with other works of art from many worlds.

"I have the original," he had said to Jon dea'Cort. "Take you the copy, and let us be in Balance."

And so it had been done, and now they were--attached to Scouts, spending time on this research station, or that surveillance ship, while Bell painted, and sketched, and fed his art. Cyra fed her own art, and her jewelry was sought after, when they came to a world where they might sell, or trade.

"We do well," she said, leaning forward to kiss his cheek. "I am pleased, Bell."

He laughed gently and leaned forward, sliding his arms around her and bringing her on to his knee.

"You're pleased, are you?" he murmured against her hair. "But could you not be--just a little--*more* pleased?"

She laughed and wrapped her arms closely around his neck, rubbing her cheek against the softness of his beard.

"Why, yes," she said, teasing him. "I might be--just a *little*--more pleased."

He laughed, and rose, bearing her with him, across their cabin to the bed.

--Standard Year 1293

The Darkling
By MH Bonham

The voices started again at 22:35, Monday, November 28, 2135. I remember the exact date only because if you're a schizophrenic, you hold onto real numbers. In the fine line between delusion and reality, sometimes holding onto something that simple is all you need to keep your sanity.

"Tell me what they say again, General?" Major Glickman asked. Typical shrink. Staring into his tablet and typing some god-awful diagnosis that would go via quantum message direct to Washington where my file on some server resides. Somewhere within that file says, *Brigadier General Martin Langley, War Hero.*

I glared at Glickman. "*They* don't say anything."

"You just said a minute ago that they started talking to you again yesterday." Glickman looked smug, his lips twisted in a wry smile and his blue eyes stared back at me. I looked closer at his pock-marked face and crewcut.

"Who the fuck did you piss off?" I muttered.

The kid scrunched his nose. "What? I asked for this assignment."

"You asked to be Marty Langley's shrink?" I shook my head. "How old are you?"

"We've been through this before, Sir. I'm 23 and I asked to be stationed on Sagittarius Omega."

"Nobody asks to get stationed to this godforsaken place." I stood up and straightened my uniform.

"We're not done with our session."

"Yes we are." I turned to leave the room, knowing there wasn't a goddamn thing the little ass could do. The suits in Washington wouldn't get their jollies today. Or tomorrow. Or whatever the fuck time or date it was on Earth.

"You know Captain Kyn is on board."

I hesitated for a moment. Kyn? Captain Stephanie Kyn, my wingman? What the hell? "Kyn? What's she's doing here?"

"I don't know—you'll have to ask her yourself." Glickman looked smug. The son-of-a-bitch knew exactly why she came here.

I should've known too, but the Voices have been intruding again. I tried to remember, but my memory blurred. Maybe something having to do with the tests on the Darkling? I couldn't remember.

*

As I walked down the drab gray corridors of the space station toward my office, I wondered what in the hell I was doing here. Occasionally one of the outpost's denizens passed me by with a quick salute and a sideways glance. They knew. They all knew their war hero was nuts. They acted the part and I acted mine, but I could tell by their sideways glances they had no confidence left.

The Chiefs of Staff should've drummed me out and left me to rot in one of their looney bins for the incurably insane, but some things you just can't do, even if your war hero is schizo. I went in for the usual treatment that cures 87 percent of the victims of the disease, but I'm one of the 13 percent who wouldn't respond. Unlucky 13 percent. Sure, the doctors hold up those odds like they've cured everyone. And they have. Except those unlucky 13 percent. Except me.

"General Langley!" A tow-headed kid wearing pilot wings saluted me. Damn if he didn't have zits. No off coloring. He looked fully human; no genetic augmentation. Damn, when did they start putting humans back in the fighter squads?

"Lieutenant…?" I scanned his badge. "Georges?"

The kid broke into a grin. "Yeah, that's me, sir! I'm here with Captain Kyn as her wingman. The Captain told me all about you and the Polaris raids. Fantastic!" He looked like he wanted to kiss me.

"That was some time ago," I replied.

"Yeah, I was ten when that happened."

Ten, un-fucking-believable. When did they make human lieutenants at 17? I forced a smile. "I'd love to chat, Lieutenant, but I have some things I have to do…"

"Right, General." Georges gave me his snappiest salute. I saluted back and headed to my office.

I wasn't on duty until 0800, but given that I commanded the Sagittarius Omega USAF007N Space Outpost, off duty was a luxury and not a given.

Spectacular doesn't describe the view from my office. It's the only

47

decent thing being way the hell out here in the middle of fucking nowhere. I've got a view of the Darkling Nebula that beats every single view in the galaxy. If you're going to be stuck on the last fucking outpost in the middle of BF Egypt, having an amazing view is a helluva consolation.

The Darkling is like nothing scientists have ever seen. Imagine the darkest nebula with some of the brightest light behind them. It is so bright that I don't even need office lights and we're a bit more than 500 lightyears away. Our engineers fitted the station with some of the best shields to ensure that all that radiation wouldn't get in, and that the light was dimmed to a bearable glare. If you look in the Darkling, itself, you see nothing but black.

Then, I heard them again. Voices. Some were low and melodious, but a few were sharp and high pitched.

Vvvvvvvvvvvvvvvbbbbbbbbbbbbbbbbbbbbbbbb

Delalalalay herewhiiiiiiiiiiiiiiii

Ffffffffffffffffffffffzzzzzzzzzzzzzzzzzzzzzkkkkkkkkkkkkkkkk

Made no goddamn sense. It sounded like another language. Maybe something that the *Kreet* would come up with. The *Verals* which we fought the last war with didn't speak like that, and I was fluent in just about all their dialects. But we were on the opposite side of the galaxy from the *Kreet*. And even if it were *Kreet*, they weren't a telepathic species. There was no fucking reason for these words to end up in my head…

I stared into the Darkling, my eyes fixed on its blackness. Somewhere between the darkness and the light, things writhed. Dark things. Sinister things.

Something cold touched my heart. I gasped for air and found it in the stale, but oxygenated ventilations.

A soft rap on the door pulled me away and the voices quieted. Not quite gone, but softer.

"General Langley?" Captain Stephanie Kyn's voice came through the comm.

"Shit, Steph, you know goddamn well it's Marty. When the hell did you show up?"

"Got here at 2100 hours. Sir, may I enter?"

"Sure, come on in."

The captain buzzed through the door with a tablet in her hands. Her darker skin and greenish cast to her hair marked her as one of the genetic variants from the Cyprus sector. Like me, she had genetic augmentations that gave her greater strength, higher intelligence, and other desirable traits in a soldier. Most of us had been from multigenerational stock, and most of us gravitated toward the armed forces. But what did a warrior do when there was no war? Sure, we were faster and stronger than the Normals, but that also made us scary. Too scary to fit in anywhere where there were Normal humans who couldn't deal with our strengths.

That's why Kyn and so many of our kind were out here. Out here and forgotten. Just like the general who hears voices.

"I don't remember hearing you arrived. Saw your wingman Lieutenant Wet-Behind-The Ears."

"You mean Georges?" She sighed. "Yeah, the kid is fresh out of the academy. Real good for a human, but passible for a mutant. He didn't offer to suck you, did he?"

"Nearly did. I thought he creamed when he saw me."

"Shit." Kyn shook her head. "I'll have a word with him."

"Don't bother. He'll get over it." I looked her over. "Damn, Steph, you look good. Peacetime has been treating you well enough."

She smiled, baring her predator fangs. It would unnerve most people, but I had seen it so much that it hardly registered. "Too soft. That's why I took the assignment."

"What assignment?"

She nodded toward the Darkling nebula. "They're getting unusual readings from the nebula. I'm here to make sure nothing weird happens."

"Babysitting the boffins, eh?" I walked over to my desk and pulled out a bottle of single malt. "Want some?"

"Sir..."

"We're off duty."

"I know that, sir. It's just not..."

"Oh fer Christ's sakes, don't tell me you've stopped drinking."

Kyn's lilac eyes went from my face to the bottle and then back.

"No, but I'm on duty."

"Fuck that." I pulled opened the drawer and pulled out two glasses. "Right now, you're off duty." I stared at the glasses in my hands. "They're a little dusty."

She grabbed them and ran them under the sonic cleaner in the wall. "Major Glickman says you left therapy."

"Glickman can stick it up his ass." The intense buzzing in my head grew worse and I could almost see the writhing darkness take form in the nebula.

"Glickman tells me you're hearing voices again."

"Glickman is getting jettisoned out an airlock."

"You don't drink as much anymore?" Kyn considered me. It had been two years since we'd seen each other, and the war already felt like another lifetime away. She looked good—she had to be in her thirties now. She was probably wondering who the worn-out old man was.

"Nah." I poured a glass and handed it to her. "Glickman's full of shit—and he shouldn't be discussing my medical file with anyone. He's violated how many laws?"

She took the glass and stared at the amber liquid. "From Earth?"

"Only the best." I downed mine with a gulp.

She took a taste. "Wow."

I nodded. "Smooth."

She gulped the whiskey and her eyes crossed for a moment. I chuckled and she grinned. "General, the scientists..."

"Marty."

"Marty," she snickered.

"What's so funny?"

"Damn, remember when you used to insist on us calling you Major Langley?"

"Yeah, that was when I was thinking I had a career in the military," I quipped.

She frowned. She set down her glass on the desk. "I better be leaving. The scientists from Sagittarius Delta should be here in twelve hours." She turned away.

"What scientists?"

"Boffins? Remember? There's been an anomaly with the Darkling

Nebula and that's got the scientific community in an uproar." She looked forlornly at the Scotch. "Thanks for the drink, General."

"Hey, Kyn…"

She turned and gave me a hard look. "You know, you shouldn't be drinking when on meds."

I stared at her, and then glanced at her glass on my desk. "What I do in my off time is my own goddamn business."

"Yes, sir."

I turned to stare at the Darkling. I could hear the voices again. The Darkling was speaking to me. Pleading to me. I poured some more Scotch and downed it. Then I poured myself another glass.

"Will that be all, sir?" Kyn's voice cut through the others. Damn it. She hadn't left, and she saw me drink that much booze.

"Yeah, Captain." I waved her away and listened to the Voices.

*

I awoke to alarms blaring throughout the station. The station shuddered; something had hit us. Looking out at the Darkling, I could see its tendrils lash out at us like a malevolent octopus. It swatted again at the station and the floor beneath me shuddered. I lurched over to my desk.

The klaxons whined. I punched the comm button. "Sergeant, what in the hell is going on?"

"General?" Sergeant Jones' face appeared on the panel. He looked puzzled, but not at all alarmed. "Is something wrong?"

I glanced at the alarm lights flashing above me. "Don't you see it? Hear it?"

"See what, General?" Jones looked concerned. "Is something wrong? Should I send for Glickman?"

"No, I just had a bad dream," I lied. If I pretended, I could almost see the station's warning lights stop. Maybe even block out the alarms. "Never mind. Carry on."

I glanced at the clock and the alarms and sirens stopped. I guess it must have been twelve hours or so since I talked to Kyn. The Darkling was still out there and still malevolent, but it was no longer reaching out for us. But I did see the small transport come out of hyperspace and turn toward the landing docks. The scientists who were all agog over the Darkling would soon be here and would be falling all over themselves to study it.

I do not wish to be studied...

I looked down at the scotch bottle. I had drained half of it while listening to the goddamn voices. I poured another glass.

You should not be here.

I took a swig and stared at the Darkling. "Who are you?"

I am sdhfkwlah, or that's what I thought it said. I couldn't tell. It was all gibberish.

"Are you the Darkling?"

The Darkling writhed. *Send the scientists home. They will harm us.*

"Us? You mean there are more than just you?"

Yes.

"What are you?" I gulped down the alcohol.

I am sdfgiiehg.

Fuck. Why couldn't it be something I could understand? Even *Kreet* made more sense. I considered refreshing my neurotrainer on some of the more esoteric languages like *Kreet*. Maybe I'd understand the words better.

I am not Kreet.

Not fucking *Kreet*. Great. What was it?

The Darkling made no reply.

I stared at the empty scotch bottle. When did I drink it all?

I frowned. Whatever it was, I was hearing it when nobody else did. That made me either enlightened or dangerously insane. I looked into the dark pit of the nebula and shook my head. Something the scientists would do would put the Darkling and everything at risk. Everything.

Kyn had come to the outpost as security. She would have enough to override my say-so and have me committed if she needed to. Not that the military hadn't already committed me to this backwater place.

I knew what I had to do. I had to stop the scientists before something big happened. I pulled up the orders on my touchpad and read through them.

Fuck. Fuck. Fuck.

I left my office and headed down the corridors toward the docking bays. Being the outpost's commander gave me complete access to everything, which is good if you're the commander. It's bad if you're the commander who is fucking insane and hears voices. I walked into the bay and looked at the craft docked alongside Bay 10. Two star fighters sat next to it that I knew had to be Kyn's and Georges'. They were small ships, they each had enough room for two pilots and maybe a passenger or so. I suspected that Kyn flew single because everyone thought this was such a low risk job. Everyone except me.

It wasn't a fighter, but a hybrid. It could carry supplies, missile, or even medicines. But it did have the fighter guns and even a turret. It also had missile pylons that housed some pretty heavy hitters. Quantum and phase plasma. Scary shit. I'd seen what those babies did first hand in our last war. There were protests against them, the way protests always happen. These missiles could blow holes in space-time if the space-time fabric was weak in the area. But our scientists had assured us that it wouldn't happen. Couldn't happen.

"General Langley?" I heard Georges' voice. I started for a brief moment and then regained my composure. It wouldn't do to show my nerves. If I were younger, a human would never had been able to pull this shit. He already had his flight suit on and looked down at his checklist on his tablet.

"That's a lovely ship." I looked at his craft. The ship's sleek lines made it look aggressive and beautiful at the same time, but it was all for PR. In space, you didn't need to worry about aerodynamics. We could be flying bricks and the ship would behave the same. No, the reason ships look cool is to get the buy-off from the head honchos. "You wouldn't mind taking an old man on the flight, would you?"

"I'm sorry, sir, but this is official business." His voice held a tinge of remorse. "How about after the study?"

I shrugged. "You don't have a co-?"

Georges nodded. "We don't need one."

"Yeah, you do. That's an order."

An unmistakable look of admiration crossed his face. If he were a puppy, I'd think it were cute. "You're rated?"

"I can be by eleven-hundred."

He glanced at the tablet's chronometer. "Okay, General, that's cutting it short. But we'll wait for you."

I nodded. "Don't tell Kyn I'm with you."

"Why not, sir?" Again the puppy dog look in his brown eyes.

"It's a surprise. She'll get a kick out of me flying with you."

"Right, sir!" He saluted and I saluted back. All too easy.

*

Back at my office, I pulled on my old flight suit, uploaded the specs and training materials, and ran a quick neurofeed. Most of the time these neurotrainers do nothing other than download information to your brain. Occasionally, someone like me wigs out and starts hearing voices, get labeled psychotic, and you get busted. Some of the shrinks seem to think that it has something to do with scrambling our brains. I think it has to do with quantum shifts. The shrinks think I'm nuts. They say there's nothing wrong with the quantum fields produced by the neurotrainers. Everyone goes through them, and no one ever has to go to a class or learn something the old fashion way, which is why they don't ban them. It almost never affects Normals—and there's only a one percent increase in those of us that are genetically modified. And even most don't consider it a risk.

After all, I'm just a soldier—bred to be a soldier. We're throwaways for our society, and we know it. So what if one point one percent of soldiers go psychotic from it? But the voices aren't my imagination. They're real. No matter what all the scans and exams fail to prove, the voices are real. It's not my fault they don't know what they are.

I click off the neurotrainer, and to my surprise, I see Glickman staring at me from the door.

"I thought I told you to avoid the neurotrainers." Glickman's voice drips with reproach.

"I thought I told you to fuck off." I pushed the trainer away, stood up, and headed to the door. "What in the hell are you doing in my office, Major?"

"Using the neurotrainer sends a signal out to my office." Glickman folded his arms. "Are you planning on flying on the mission?"

"So what?"

"In case you hadn't checked your medical records lately, General, you're grounded."

"By who?"

"Me." Glickman looked smug. "You're still hearing voices, and you're using that neurotrainer like hits from a crack pipe. It's already scrambled your brains enough, hasn't it?"

I looked at Glickman and frowned. I hated seeing the guy look so smug. So when I crossed the room faster than any normal human could and hit him with a stunner, he didn't even have time to react. That's one of the problems with being genetically augmented. You don't even get to wipe the smug look from their faces when you take them down.

"Nighty-night, moron." I closed the door and dragged the shrink behind my desk. The rise and fall of his chest told me he still lived, but he'd suffer a helluva headache and he'd be sore all over for about a week. Good.

I walked out to the docking bays.

*

Georges looked up from his touchpad as he stood near the ship waiting for me. "That was quick."

I glanced at the time. "You didn't believe it would take 15 minutes?"

He shrugged. "The main trainers take close to an hour."

"This is an XK1128. All I needed was a refresh on piloting and differences between that and the XKN-72." I flashed the ratings on the pad.

"Good, let's go."

At that moment, Kyn appeared from under her wing. "What are you doing here?"

"Playing tourist with the Kid." I pointed a thumb at Georges who hesitated as he climbed the ladder into the ship.

"That okay, Captain?" Georges glanced from Kyn to me in confirmation.

"I would've given you a ride as co-," Kyn remarked. "You feeling a bit itchy to fly?"

"Yeah," I said, feeling relieved that my cover wasn't blown. "I know you're busy, so I thought I'd give the kid a break."

"You cleared?" Kyn glanced at her pad.

"Yeah, check the logs—Glickman cleared me today." Funny what a passkey and Level 1 security can do. I had returned the passkey on Glickman when I finished using it. Hopefully he'd stay passed out for a few hours.

We climbed aboard. I took the second-in-command's seat as Georges went through his primary checklist. I went through the secondary checklist and frowned. The Voices had been quiet, but I got the feeling of anticipation from them. Could this be another delusion? Could I be wrong?

We launched and headed into the Darkling's inky blackness.

*

I scanned the mission briefs while we flew. The scientists had already sent in quantum probes but had no response. The Darkling looked bigger to me. *It's your imagination,* I told myself. Could the probes have done that much damage to the space-time continuum in this section of the universe? The universe was fragile here—fragile beyond words. Without careful management, the two universes would start to unravel where they touched.

The seating in this hybrid fighter allowed side-by-side controls in the cockpit. Old style fighters usually were one person, or two people, but the two person fighters had a forward and an aft. The pilot sat in fore and a weapon's officer sat behind.

The scientists would send in a science drone. Little did they know they had enough probes to detonate the space-time continuum, if they reached the Darkling.

"Oh look, there it is." Kyn's voice over the radio broke me from my reverie. I looked up and saw the science drone with a number of probes hanging off the sides like a weird porcupine.

"Scanners," I muttered.

"What?" Georges glanced at me. "What are you saying?"

"They have quantum phase scanners."

"Of course, how else would they scan the anomaly?"

Of course they would. I felt the shudder of the thing within the Darkling. I knew what I had to do. I pointed the stunner at Georges.

"I'm sorry," I said as I pulled the trigger.

"Gen—" With that, the bolt of energy hit him square in the face and zipped down him.

Georges slumped in his chair. His breathing told me he was still alive. He'd be okay, assuming we pulled through this. I felt sorry for the kid. Helluva way to meet your hero. I took a deep breath and took the controls. I patched his intercom into mine.

I lied when I said I hadn't flown XK1128 hybrids. I had 7000 hours pilot-in-command on them. The fifteen minutes were to teach me how to reroute the controls and the weapons command to me alone. I took control of the aircraft and pitched it downward toward the science drone.

"Lieutenant, you're off course." Kyn's voice came from the radio.

"Sorry kiddo," I muttered and hit the burners. The hybrid raced toward the Darkling, but the science drone had quite a lead on us already. We were here just to observe and make sure the probes didn't cause anything stupid.

"What the fuck?" Kyn's voice rattled in my ears. "Marty, what's happening?"

"Sorry Steph," I said. "This mission has to stop."

"What the—Marty, put Georges on line."

I glanced at Georges. His head lolled to one side. "Sorry, kiddo, he's taking a nap."

"What the fuck did you do, Langley?" Steph's voice came out in her no-nonsense "you're going to eat shit and die" tone.

"You know, Steph, he's kinda young. He needed a nap. So I gave him one."

"What the fuck are you doing?"

"Saving the universe, I hope." I dove toward the science drone as it made its way toward utter destruction. Kyn was hot on my tail. I had to give it to her, I couldn't shake her. I tuned into the main com to hear Kyn talking to Control.

"... gone schizo on me—he's incapacitated my wingman and headed toward the Explorer...Over," Kyn said.

"Don't let him near the Explorer. It's got sensitive equipment. Over" Control grated in my ears.

"Hell, I think he's going to destroy it. Over."

"Captain, this is mission critical. Get him back. Over."

"You got a cut switch? I can't pull him back..."

"We're contacting Central Command to get permission to fire on them to disable them."

"But that might kill both of them. The drone doesn't have anyone on board. You're going to kill two people to save a drone?"

*

I shut off the comm. I had already reprogrammed the cut routines; they'd be useless. It's standard procedure for any fighter jock because you didn't want the enemy to leave you dead in space. The problem was when someone went loco. The question was whether Kyn would fire on us. To disable, not destroy, but sometimes you went out in a blaze of glory. I hit the thrusters and fired my blasters into the science drone.

The thing lit off like one of the arc lights you see footage of in old time war footage. "Holy shit," I said as I tried to shield my eyes from the blast. "What the fuck did they have on board?"

I didn't have time to answer my own question.

*

The Darkling came alive and opened up, reaching out with its dark tentacles and swallowing my hybrid like it was a tasty snack. We spun wildly and I was sure I'd lose whatever I had left in my stomach. At one point, I felt like taffy, being pulled and stretched.

"Fuck it, Marty! What the hell is happening?" Kyn shouted in my comm.

"Captain, do you read? This is Control, we lost your signal, ov..."

I'm pretty sure I screamed.

Somewhere along the way I fell unconscious.

When I awoke, I was standing in darkness. It wasn't night because I could see my body and hands without a problem. Everything else was black. I looked around and to my surprise, both Kyn and Georges were standing next to me. They, too, were clearly visible.

"Where are we?" Georges spoke first, his voice very small.

"Fuck if I know," Kyn said. "We're probably dead."

"Dead!" Georges' voice went up an octave and he turned paler than before. He pulled off his helmet and ran a hand through his sweat-soaked hair. "Shit! I'm dead? I'm dead! Oh my god! I'm…"

That's when I punched him in the mouth. He fell backward in surprise and landed on his butt. On something. Something that we were standing on.

"Ow! That hurt!" he shouted.

"Not dead," I noted when he wiped his mouth and a trickle of blood oozed out. I looked at Kyn who smirked. "What's so funny?"

"I can't help but think of the time when you did that at a bar in Gamma Four."

I snorted. "Yeah, I got away with a lot." I frowned. "So if we're not dead, why are we here?" I looked around.

"We…are…Darkling." The Voices I had heard in my head now boomed through the darkness.

"Where the fuck are we?" Kyn asked.

"Bubble of Space-Time. Yours…"

"We're in a bubble of our universe's space-time?" I mused. "But we're not in our universe."

"No."

"Where are we?" Kyn asked, glancing at me, worriedly.

"The Darkling must've accidentally pulled us in when I closed the rip in the two Universes."

"We're in another universe?" Kyn stated, looking around in disbelief.

"This is our little section of space-time—otherwise we'd explode," I said.

"Correct." The Darkling boomed around us.

Georges whimpered.

"Where's our ships?" Kyn asked.

I looked up—even though I couldn't see the disembodied Voices, it felt right to do so. "I think we're still in them. I think we're in what we might call a mass hallucination. It's how they communicate, Steph. These beings in a different universe with different laws of physics have figured out a way to contact us through the gaps—the weak spots of the Universes, where they rub."

"Correct," the Voices said.

"They've been trying to talk to people who are sensitive to their communications for eons. These people have been misinterpreting them because our brains have had no common frame of reference. So, we've been called 'crazy' and 'psychotic.'"

"Correct," the Voices said.

"This close to the Darkling—the rift—I understood what they were trying to tell me. The quantum phase scanners and analyzers would make the rift worse. The scientists were on the verge of destroying both universes."

"Why didn't they—whoever is here—stop them?"

"They can't enter our Universe either. We just lucked out that with the explosion, some of our Universe got trapped in a bubble."

"We maintain for a little while, and then send you back."

"You can do that?" Kyn asked.

"Took long. Scientists took many iaushffffffffffffffff..."

"What was that?" Kyn looked at me.

"Something not translatable. Maybe a time unit. I got those blips when I started hearing words at first. Now, they can at least translate."

"Took long." The Voice agreed.

"Are we going back?" Georges asked.

"Yes, now." The Voices agreed. "Darkling no longer there."

"They closed the rift. We're the last part of it." I looked at Kyn. Our universe is safe there.

"Yes..." the Voices said.

With that, I fell unconscious.

*

I awoke in a hospital bed with monitor bleeping merrily. The room was dark, but I would recognized the antiseptic smell anywhere. "Fuck, would someone get me a drink?"

"I tried to sneak in some whiskey, but they wouldn't let me." A light turned on and I blinked, momentarily blinded.

"Kyn?" My eyes adjusted and saw my old Captain wingman, now dressed in civies. It looked like hospital scrubs to my eyes.

"Yeah, they released me two days ago, but they said you were still out."

"How…?"

"First, you're on Centaurus 5. They found our ships floating where the Darkling had been and brought us all to the nearest planet with Class 1 medical facilities. The Darkling is gone. It imploded when we got sucked in and a short time later, our ships got spat out. The physicists are having a heyday with this. Seems there's enough quantum shifting to detect traces of the other universe. The boffins are saying that the Darkling was a rip in the fabric of space-time. You were hearing voices from the other side.

"They grilled the lieutenant first and then after I woke up, they grilled me too. Seems our stories corroborate. Everyone is hailing you as a hero, having saved two universes." She crossed her arms and looked smug at me. "Actually all three of us are heroes—but you should hear how Georges talks about you. The kid is going to follow you around like a puppy forever."

I groaned. "No whiskey?"

Kyn shook her head. "They'll want your side of the story, but they're pretty sure you'll say the same things. Anyway, it's all being recorded so if you say anything special, they'd want to hear it. But no, Glickman says no whiskey."

"Glickman? Isn't that ass demoted yet?"

"Hell, no. He's been extoled for his work with those who have abilities to sense other universes in space-time rifts. He's publishing a paper on it and may get a promotion."

"Great. Fucking great."

"Don't worry, you're getting promoted too." Kyn said. "You're a three star general now."

"A what?" I said.

"You'll be getting a helluva raise." She grinned. "I'm now a major for not having blown up your ship."

"You know, you disobeyed orders." I gave her my sternest look.

She laughed. "Yeah, well, sometimes you have to ignore those orders."

"Who in the hell taught you that?" I closed my eyes.

"I don't know. Maybe from some schizo general who heard voices?" Kyn gave my arm a squeeze. "I'll let you rest. Tomorrow, let's have lunch. They have the shittiest coffee in the cafeteria here."

"It's a date," I said as I listened to her leave, relishing in the first real silence I had in a long time.

A Vanishing Past
By David Lee Summers

Captain Ellison Firebrandt sat dozing in his wood-paneled cabin aboard the privateer *Legacy*, a half-empty glass of wine on the desk beside him and smooth jazz on the speakers. The ship had just completed a lucrative mission and orbited Earth. Most of the crew enjoyed shore leave on the planet below. A knock at the door roused him.

"Come in," he said.

A woman with long, black hair and deep brown eyes wearing a form-fitting dress entered.

"Miss Suki," remarked the captain. "I thought you would be planetside with the rest of the crew."

Suki Mori stepped over to a cabinet and retrieved a glass. She helped herself to the captain's wine and sat down in a chair across from him, then swallowed a gulp. "I'd really like to see my parents."

The captain frowned. Over the last few months, he began to think of Suki as more than a member of his crew. She was a friend and confidant. Perhaps she could be more, but strengthening their relationship would also increase his vulnerability.

"They're on Ceres. Roberts—" Suki referred to the first mate "—tells me it's only a few hours away in the solar system's current alignment."

The captain remained silent, eyes half closed as he contemplated his relationship with the dwarf planet in the asteroid belt between Mars and Jupiter.

Suki took another gulp of wine. "Surely you know by now you can trust me. I don't plan to run away."

Firebrandt's lips tilted upward in a faint smile. There was a time she would have run. Even now, she didn't seem entirely comfortable making a living raiding other ships. He took a drink, then shook his head. "It's not a matter of trusting you or of distance. Ceres is … difficult for me to visit."

"How so?"

Firebrandt poured a fresh glass of wine and stared into the distance. Finally, he took a sip. "My father lives on Ceres."

Suki's breath caught. "You've never told me about your father. Is he a mineralogist?"

The captain shook his head sadly. He wished he could take as much pride in his father as Suki did her scientist parents. "Just a miner."

"Nothing wrong with that. Does he make a good living?" Suki sipped her wine.

Firebrandt snorted. "The money's adequate for his needs. Living?" The captain shrugged. How could he explain without revealing more about himself than he wanted? By the same token, he saw no reason to deny her request. He reached over and activated the intercom. "Mr. Roberts, think the skeleton crew would mind a little field trip over to Ceres? We can pick up some fuel while we're there and Miss Suki has requested shore time."

"You should take some for yourself, Captain," suggested the first mate.

The captain narrowed his gaze and frowned. The first mate also knew about his father, but avoided making a more direct suggestion. A knot formed in the captain's stomach. "Set out when ready."

"Thank you." Suki finished her wine and stood up. As she strode past the captain, she stopped, bent over and kissed him on his cheek. He felt his face warm but willed himself not to react further. The walls had already crumbled too much.

*

Firebrandt waited by AB Mining Co's airlock in the Dantu pressure dome on Ceres. A bored man with several days' stubble walked up to a control board and checked some stats, then looked up. "Can I help you?"

"My father is Bradbury Firebrandt. He's working the shift that gets off soon."

The man at the control board grunted and returned his attention to his work. Fifteen minutes later, a light next to the airlock cycled from red to green and the airlock rolled open with a hiss. Several men and women wearing dust-encrusted space suits passed through. Most unclasped their helmets the moment they stepped through the door.

One figure continued through the staging area toward the locker room. The man at the console smiled, shook his head and jogged over to the man. "Brad!" He shouted so the man could hear through the helmet. "Your son is here."

The man turned around and finally reached up and unclasped his helmet. He lifted it off and narrowed his gaze. His face was very much like the captain's with deeper furrows. White stubble covered his face and the top of his head as though someone had simply taken a razor and cut it all to the same length. "Home from school, boy?"

Ellison Firebrandt smiled in spite of himself. "It's been a long time since I've been in school, dad. Get out of that suit and I'll walk you home."

The old man's brow furrowed, but he nodded and disappeared into the locker room. Fifteen minutes later, he reappeared, this time wearing a pair of orange coveralls, frayed at the cuffs and worn at the knees and elbows. He turned right and entered a tunnel without stopping for his son.

Ellison hurried to catch up with him. "Thought you were going to leave without me?"

The old man turned his head, eyes narrowed. A moment later he brightened. "Home from school, boy? You need a haircut."

The captain grimaced then self-consciously ran his hands through his long, red hair. His father suffered from dementia, though the mining operators never bothered to determine its exact cause. It could be Alzheimer's or he might have suffered a mini-stroke, or any number of other conditions. Despite the dementia, his father's muscles knew how to operate laser drills and sonic blasters. The mine company had invested money in augmenting those same muscles with nanofibers to keep them strong. They just couldn't be bothered to invest in diagnosing his mind and even a fairly successful privateer captain didn't make enough to send his father to a quality neuroclinic for further evaluation. "I've been out of school for a long time," said Ellison. "My ship's orbiting Ceres. I'm taking some shore leave."

"Quit school, did you?" asked Bradbury.

"Finished school a long time ago," said Ellison. "I'm captain of a ship now."

The old man's brow furrowed. "Seen anything of your mother?"

Ellison snorted. "I'm the one who doesn't remember her."

Bradbury nodded slowly. "That's right. She run off when you were a baby." He looked off into the distance. "Barbara was so beautiful, but she always had itchy feet and big dreams. She never liked being the wife of a miner."

They entered a corridor and passed several doors. Finally, Bradbury stopped and blinked several times. He extracted an electronic key from his pocket and tried it on the locking plate of the nearest door. The key and the plate both blinked red.

Ellison gently took the key from his father's hand. It had the number 13 on it even though they stood before apartment 15. "I think we passed it by one."

They walked back a door and Ellison tried the key. The door opened to a neat little one-room apartment. "Good afternoon, Brad," chimed the computer. "Your afternoon medication has been dispensed. Please let me know what you'd like for dinner."

"Gimme a hamburger and a chocolate shake."

The computer paused a moment. "Will add suitable nutrients to bring requested food up to appropriate dietary standards."

"Yeah, yeah, whatever." Bradbury crossed the room to the small kitchen nook, retrieved the pills and some water and swallowed them down. When finished, he looked up at his son. "Ellison? How nice to see you. Home from school?"

The question was getting old. "Just visiting. I'm here with my ship, the *Legacy*. Roberts is aboard keeping an eye on her."

"Robert? Who's Robert?"

"Just my best friend since my days in the merchant service."

"Merchant service? When did you join the merchant service? Did you quit school?"

The captain rubbed the bridge of his nose. Every time he visited his father, he felt like a piece of his own past vanished. His father remembered his mother—the mother who abandoned them both—with clarity, but he could barely remember the son who stuck with him for sixteen years after she left.

"Would you like something to eat?" asked the old man.

Ellison sighed. He'd had enough synthesized food over the last several weeks. "I'll take a salmon salad with spinach leaves and onions, drizzled with a light vinaigrette."

"Not your kind of food at all," remarked Bradbury. "You hate vegetables."

"I *hated* vegetables … when I was a kid."

Soon, a wall panel opened delivering the food for both men. Bradbury took a seat on a tattered sofa, while Ellison sat in an adjoining chair. They each lifted tabletops built into the furniture. Bradbury turned on the holo screen, letting a news channel play while they ate.

"So you say you're aboard a ship now?" The old man took a bite of his burger, then focused on the chocolate milk shake. He took a sip, made a face, then took another sip.

"I own a ship. I call her the *Legacy*."

"Nice name. Freighter?"

"We haul cargo from time to time." The captain hesitated discussing his career as a privateer captain in depth. He hated to expend the energy explaining something his father would forget in ten minutes.

Satisfied with the brief explanation, the old man returned to his burger. He finished about half of it, then lit a cigarette. He sat back, and watched the news for a while, then turned to Ellison and smiled. "It's good to see you, son. You say you're aboard a ship now?"

Ellison sighed. "Yes, the *Legacy*."

Bradbury nodded, oblivious to having heard the answer recently. "Gotta be careful when you captain a ship here in the asteroid belt. Accidents happen."

The captain's brow furrowed. The conversation had taken an interesting turn. "What kind of accidents?"

"You remember Mathilde?"

Firebrandt thought back. He remembered a rundown pressure dome and kids who called him a shrimp. He learned to fight on the asteroid Mathilde. "Miserable little hunk of rock," muttered the captain.

"Remember that big crater? Scientists used to think another asteroid collided with it—reasonable in the belt—but sonic imaging found something else. We found a Rd'dyggian treasure galleon down there. Old one, too. They used to make their currency out of rhodium. We found huge heaps of it in the hold."

Ellison looked up from his salad. "The ship was intact? How did it survive the crash?"

Bradbury shrugged. "They must have screwed up their hyperspace jump calculations and plowed right into the asteroid before they jumped fully into the beyond. We made a tunnel, but we were only able to get a few of the rhodium coins out."

The captain reached into his coat pocket and retrieved a pipe and tobacco pouch. An ancient Rd'dyggian galleon would be worth a small fortune, especially if it still held a cargo of rhodium coins. "Couldn't you blast it out of the rock?" He began packing the pipe.

The old man shook his head. "The ship was too fragile. We'd have destroyed it if we tried to blast. Besides, that would have drawn attention to the ship. We weren't about to tell the mine owners, or else they'd claim everything for themselves."

Ellison Firebrandt lifted his pipe to his mouth and lit it. He smoked for a few minutes, thinking. The *Legacy's* crew recently happened upon a nodal point generator, which let them perform short interspatial jumps while in the solar system. The experimental device might just be used to extract the galleon from the asteroid. "If I took you to Mathilde, do you think you could lead us to the tunnel you made?"

"Are you kidding? I remember it like it was yesterday."

They turned their attention to the news for a while. His pipe finished, Ellison stood and collected his father's dishes. The old man blinked at his son, startled.

"Ellison? Home from school?"

The captain closed his eyes, feeling vulnerable despite the excitement of the quest.

*

The asteroid Mathilde expanded to fill the *Legacy's* holographic viewer. The captain pointed to a large depression on the asteroid's surface. "Scan there and see if you can find evidence for this ship my father's talking about."

The man known as Computer closed his eyes for a moment. When he opened them, they drifted back and forth. Finally, they locked on the captain. "There's a hollow space under the crater, like a small cavern."

A three-dimensional schematic appeared, overlaid on the asteroid's image. Roberts crossed his arms over his barrel chest and shook his head. "Doesn't prove anything. It could be a natural cavern that formed under the crater somehow."

"Unlikely," responded Computer. "Mathilde is composed of metal-rich carbonaceous chondrites. Few natural caves have been recorded."

Firebrandt nodded. "Compare the cavern to schematics we have of old Rd'dyggian galleons circa twelve hundred years ago."

A series of ship schematics appeared in the holographic viewer. One separated from the others and oriented itself over the cavern. The area and shape were a near perfect match. The captain nodded slowly as he stepped over to the intercom and called the engine room. "Suki, have you disconnected the nodal point generator from the engine?"

"Almost there," she said. "It should be ready to go in about fifteen minutes."

"Perfect. Let me know when you're ready and meet me in the launch bay."

"You know, I told my parents I got a job with a space salvage company."

Firebrandt barked a laugh. "In this case, that may not be far from the truth."

"My dad says I should ask for a raise," said Suki.

"Parents are like that." The captain turned off the intercom.

Roberts approached. "So, what exactly do you plan to do? Even if you do find a twelve-hundred-year-old ship buried in the asteroid, it's not like it'll have a working engine. The ship can't jump from where it is."

Firebrandt grinned and patted Roberts on the shoulder. "The ship won't have to jump. The nodal point generator will allow the ship to drop into the beyond for a time. We'll just let the asteroid continue its orbit. The generator will disable itself after about half an hour. The ship should appear in normal space where Mathilde had been."

Roberts blinked at the captain, then ran his hand over his bald head. "That's either the most brilliant or the craziest idea I've ever heard."

"You're not going to try to stop me?"

Roberts shrugged. "If you're right, we could have a small fortune. If you're wrong, I guess I'm in command of the *Legacy*. I don't see how I lose."

*

On Mathilde, a domed ghost town called Brisbane huddled near the crater Damodar's vertex. The air generation plant had been shut down years ago. Roberts shuttled Suki along with Ellison and Bradbury Firebrandt to the surface, where they donned space suits and hiked across the surface. Roberts returned to the *Legacy*.

Captain Firebrandt pointed out places where someone had taken potshots at the transparent dome, leaving scorched holes.

"This place was always a dump," said Bradbury. "The mines played out in just a few years."

The old man led the way through a hole in the dome where an airlock had been cannibalized. Suki carried the nodal point generator in a chest pack, which counterbalanced the air pack on her back. Though heavy in normal gravity, it was easy to manage in the minimal gravity of the potato-shaped space rock. As they walked through the old town, Bradbury pointed out places he remembered. "There's the old general store." He turned around. "I used to live in an apartment up that street. I wonder if it's still there."

The captain studied the abandoned buildings. The faint light of the distant sun cast long shadows. Despite the eerie setting, Ellison smiled at his father's apparent lucidity. He seemed much more in the moment than he had in earlier conversations. "We don't have much time. Do you remember the way to the tunnel that leads to the abandoned ship?"

Bradbury's brow furrowed. "We need to get into the mine." He led the way to the center of town where a metal pillbox-shaped building stood. The old man tried the handle but found it locked.

Ellison motioned for him to stand clear. He drew his sidearm and blasted the locking mechanism. He leaned on the door and pushed it into a dark space. The captain's helmet lamp illuminated a lifting platform. He wondered if there was any way to supply power to it.

His father stepped forward and eyed the elevator. Stepping on, he opened a hatch in the bottom of the floor and shone his helmet lamp on a set of wall rungs. "The personnel lift broke down a lot. We had to climb down all too often. Sometimes we'd sneak aboard the oar lift outside the dome. They never let that one break down."

With that, the three clambered through the hatch and climbed down into the subasteroidal chambers. At the third level down, Bradbury paused. "Most of the time I worked here. I wonder if any of our old gear is still around."

"You were going to show us the way to the tunnel," said the captain.

"Tunnel?"

"Yes, the tunnel that led to the buried treasure galleon."

A silence ensued which lasted long enough that Ellison began to question the quest's sanity. Could his father focus long enough to see the mission through?

"How did you know that?" asked Bradbury. "We never told anyone about the ship we found. There's no way to get it out."

"You told me about it yesterday," said Ellison. "Just lead the way."

"We should go take the equipment lift. That always has power," remarked the old man.

"Not anymore," said Suki. "Nothing has power here."

"I wonder why that is." The old man continued climbing down the ladder. As they climbed, the only sounds Ellison heard were the rhythmic steps on the metal rungs and labored breathing transmitted through the suit speakers. The captain's muscles began to burn. He knew his father's nano-muscular implants would allow him to keep going, but he worried about Suki. They climbed past several dozen levels until they dismounted on rough laser-carved rock.

The captain looked up and estimated they'd climbed down nearly a kilometer. There was no way they could have endured the climb in Earth's gravity. Firebrandt felt warm and assumed it was from the exertion of the climb since there was no atmosphere to transfer the small amount of heat generated from subsurface pressure.

"I've only been down here a couple of times," remarked Bradbury. "Usually I worked up on the third level, but some of my friends showed me the ship they'd found down here. Did I tell you about that?"

"Yes, dad, you did," said the captain. "Can you show us which way it is?"

Bradbury Firebrandt looked around, then pointed to a tunnel that led away behind them. "We should have taken the equipment lift. It always has power."

"Nothing has power right now," said Ellison.

They followed the tunnel past abandoned laser drills and emptied emergency medical kits. Finally, they came to a place where a large steel sheet painted with graffiti leaned against the wall. "Help me with this," said the old man.

The captain grabbed one end and his father took the other and they hefted it to the side. The captain sensed his father actually took most of the weight. He began to think nano-muscular implants could be handy. A narrow tunnel twisted downward.

"The geologists discovered the ship when they were doing scans. They thought they'd found a cavern, but what really grabbed their attention was the erdonium deposit." The old man referred to the metal used to build starship hulls.

"The erdonium must have been from the hull of the Rd'dyggian ship," remarked Suki.

"How do you know about the Rd'dyggian ship?" asked Bradbury. "I never told anyone about it. Didn't think they'd believe me."

Ellison ignored his father and led the way down the winding, twisting tunnel until it opened into a large area. He saw exposed deck plating canted at a sharp angle. Across the way, strapped into a dust-covered chair were the mummified remains of a seven-foot tall Rd'dyggian warrior with a hole in his chest. Trapped in the asteroid with atmosphere failing, he no doubt took his own life rather than await suffocation or starvation. The captain shivered in spite of himself.

"These old ships used to carry coins made out of rhodium," said Bradbury, repeating information he'd relayed back on Ceres.

Suki retrieved a portable scanner from her belt. "I do detect rhodium in the holds." She shook her head. "A lot of the erdonium hull plating is gone, though. It's like whoever found this cut it out from the inside as much as possible."

"Erdonium brings in more money than rhodium," explained the old man, nothing wrong with his professional knowledge. He led the way up the canted and buckled deck of the Rd'dyggian treasure galleon to a door that had been forced open. Inside sat a small fortune in rhodium doubloons spilled against the near wall.

Ellison Firebrandt smiled.

"If most of the hull plating is gone, how do we get this ship out of here? Won't the coins just drift away?" Suki closed her porta-scanner and placed it back into its carrying case.

"The nodal point generator just creates a field. Make sure the field includes the surrounding rock. I'm sure a museum will be interested in this ship and the cargo," said the captain.

"Help me with this pack," said Suki.

The captain helped her lift off the carrying case. Despite the low gravity, it proved awkward work balanced between the wall and floor of the trapped alien vessel. They extracted the nodal point generator. Ellison pulled off his own chest pack and produced a small portable power supply. They connected it and Suki began programming. "I wouldn't recommend staying aboard the ship when the field activates. Without the erdonium plating, the radiation from the EQ-field could be deadly. How long should we allow to get out of here?"

"How far away do we need to be?" asked the captain.

"I'd like to be at the top of the ladder and out in the mining camp, at least," said Suki.

"Set it for two hours."

She set the timer and then looked up. "Okay. Time to get going."

With that, the captain looked around for his father. He was no longer in the room with them. "Dad?" called the captain. There was no response.

Suki pulled out her porta-scanner. "He's not in the ship, but the surrounding rock is making other readings difficult."

"Could he be...?" Ellison hated to speak the rest of the question.

"No. I'd still read his suit if he were dead."

The captain blew out a breath, then nodded. He motioned for Suki to follow. His dad must be out in the mines somewhere. He only hoped they would catch up to him before it was too late. They followed the winding tunnel back up to the main part of the mine then returned to the elevator shaft. Suki scanned again but didn't get any readings.

Firebrandt looked around and considered his father's words. He could imagine his father returning to the third level where he once worked, or even to the surface to try to find the old apartment. Searching either location would take a while. Just then, he remembered the ore lift. He looked around. Besides the dead-end tunnel they exited, there was only one other tunnel on the bottom level. Firebrandt followed it with Suki on his tail.

A thousand feet down the tunnel, Suki scanned again. "I register a human life form just ahead."

Firebrandt smiled and bounded forward in the low gravity. They found Bradbury Firebrandt at the ore lift, fumbling with some corroded battery leads, trying to get the lift operational again. He'd just reached out to remove the gauntlet when the captain put his hand on his dad's forearm.

"We don't have much time," warned Suki.

"Can we get this lift operational?" asked the captain.

Suki scanned the battery. "It does have some charge left." She reached into her pouch and took out a small tool that let her grab the wires and attach them to the lift controls. Once done, she threw the lever and blew out a breath when the ore lift started moving. It came down to their level and stopped.

The three climbed aboard and Bradbury threw the lever and the lift carried them toward the surface. "We used to use this lift when the main elevator would break down," he said.

*

"Ellison! Home from school?"

Ellison Firebrandt stood outside his father's apartment on Ceres. A woman in a green lab coat stood next to him.

"Who is this? A new girlfriend?"

Ellison and the woman smiled at each other as Bradbury Firebrandt stood aside and indicated they should enter. "Dad, this is Dr. Apolinaria Apodaca. She'll be looking in on you from time to time."

The doctor lifted a medical scanner. "May I?"

Bradbury Firebrandt's eyes shifted nervously from side to side. "I don't have money for a doctor's visit, especially not a house call."

"Oh yes you do," said Ellison. The Rd'dyggians paid a tidy sum for the remains of the craft salvaged from the interior of Mathilde. Embarrassed that one of their captains would steer a ship into an asteroid even twelve hundred years ago, they were willing to pay to make that part of their past vanish. They didn't even question why the holds had been emptied of the ancient rhodium coins, probably assuming the miners who stripped the vessel of its plating had emptied the hold years before. Firebrandt had already sold a few on the collectors' market and figured he'd parcel out the rest as needed in the years to come.

Dr. Apodaca looked up from her scan. "Mr. Firebrandt, may we sit."

"Of course," said the captain and miner together. They all shared a chuckle.

"You're suffering the degenerative effects of Alzheimer's. I can slow it down, possibly stop it, although I don't think I can undo any damage that's already been done."

Bradbury's eyes sharpened. "Is that why I keep saying the same thing over and over again?"

The doctor nodded.

"Do what you can to help me out."

She opened a pouch, attached a vial to a hypo and pointed it at his arm. A faint ping indicated the medication had been injected into his bloodstream. "That should help."

"Dr. Apodaca will check on you once a week. I also have a housing agent who will help you find some nicer quarters," said the captain. "If you decide you want to retire, they'll even help you move back to Earth."

Bradbury Firebrandt sniffed. "Thank you, son. I don't know how you can afford all this."

The captain snorted, glad most of his crew had been on shore leave and had no idea how much money the captain had acquired when he extracted the ancient, alien galleon. "You earned it all yourself, dad. I'll look in on you when I'm back this way in a few months."

Bradbury blinked a few times and nodded. "You're not in school anymore, are you?"

"No," said the captain.

"Be careful out there and I'll try to hold onto my memories."

Captain Firebrandt smiled and pulled his father into a hug, feeling a little less vulnerable, hopeful that his own past had ceased to vanish.

Sparks Out
By Nicole Givens Kurtz

The District's rain drenched streets and crumbling infrastructures drowned between the constant downpour. Fawn Granger marched along the soaked sidewalks in her goulashes. As a kid she liked splashing in the cold rain, feeling the spray against her naked legs. On the way to the scene, she'd reveled in the exhilaration as she puddle jumped along the cracked and warped sidewalks of the District's sectors. Overhead, the cold afternoon squall held hints of a future snowfall once the temperature plummeted below freezing.

The sky could tell her everything except the identity of the rotting corpse that awaited her at the violation scene.

Tonight she'd twisted her dreadlocks into a bun at the base of her neck. It kept her shoulder-length hair out of the way of the *body*. Nothing like getting blood, bile, and human baseness in your locks and the hell it took to get out.

"The neighbor said the death cries could be heard just after 4." Briscoe announced as soon as she crossed the yellow cautionary beam.

Briscoe Baker, B.B., an inspector for the District's Regulators, stood over the deceased. He carried an umbrella in one hand, and a cigarette in the other. He'd come prepared for the weather with a dark gray coat, black turtleneck, and dark dress pants. He didn't fit with the flying wautos—wind automobiles, robotic servers floating around the violation scene's parameter, and flutter of photographers. He looked like he'd stepped out of the Robert B. Parker's online detective game's character list.

"Really B.B. Smoking?" Fawn bent down to inspect the person who used to be alive. He wore a large, lasergun blast to the chest and regular clothing.

The violation scene techs buzzed around in their bright yellow coats that read VIO on the backs in black, block lettering. Their equipment was waterproof, but not the body.

"Can we get some protection over here? All of our evidence is running down the drain!" Fawn stood up.

"Yeah! Sorry!" shouted a male with an Afro of curls, one of the techs. He set up the two electronic devices on either side of the body. With a press of the buttons, a force field appeared like a dome. Rain ran over it and down the sides, away from the deceased.

She caught Briscoe frowning at her. His pursed lips forced the corners of his mouth downward.

"The ashes can contaminate the scene. We've talked about this."

"I'm cutting back." He took a drag as if to prove his point.

"Who is this?" Fawn gestured.

"Leonardo Cho, scientist with the Association of Genetically Engineered Humans." Briscoe took another long drag.

"And?"

"And that's it. No wife. No husband. No kids. Extended family is out in the Tokyscio area. The Cali Province is always changing the names on those damn quadrants…" He caught himself and straightened out his coat. The ash fell into the rain puddles.

"How'd he get here?" Fawn's rain-soaked pants had plastered themselves to her thighs. Great.

Briscoe shrugged. "Gonna have to wait for the vioTechs to get their work done."

"Let's talk to his employer."

"See now, Fawn, I know the place looks progressive, but there is still some backwardness to how they do things," Briscoe explained. He twisted lips as if the words tasted bad.

"I'm well aware of the things they do." Fawn heard the sharpness in her tone, but she wanted this resolved tonight. If the e-file journalists got hold of it, some tabloid snot like Malcolm Moore would ruin it. "And *backward* doesn't begin to cover it. Cruel. Deadly. Those adjectives would do."

"This is politically sensitive." He loosely crossed his arms where he could still hold the umbrella and smoke.

"I'm not speaking things you don't already know about." Fawn met his eyes and watched him squirm beneath her gaze.

"They're a not-for-profit medical *organization* whose primary focus is to enrich human beings through genetic manipulation. They conducted research to save lives and to create them." Briscoe countered.

"You write their damn website babble?" Fawn shook her head. The smell of death made her stomach hurt, but thankfully, the rain had washed out most of the odor.

"No, but life isn't about finding yourself, but about creating yourself. The AEGH creates people."

"Oh, I wonder what else they've created."

Briscoe leveled his gaze at her. "Not all of us can fly off into the Southwest."

"Is that what you're put-out about?"

"You're splitting up our successful team-up. For a ranch."

She couldn't deal with this tonight. The District had drained her. Eight years had rendered her sparks out. They'd labeled her with the PTSD, and leaving the District would move her from the trauma of regulator life. Her mother had been a regulator. She'd told Fawn when she first rookied for the District about the dangers of trying to shovel humanity's muck. It could cover you, and drown out one's spirit, their spark.

Burn. Explode. Ignite. Spark. But don't get snuffed out.

The bodies. She couldn't stop seeing them, even when asleep.

"I'm not going to go through it again. This is our last one, so let's make it count."

She didn't want to go through this again. Without waiting for Briscoe's reply, she started for the supervising vioTech. They needed answers.

She also wanted to stop him from going on about the AEGH. They created hatchlings. In fact, Briscoe, being a hatchling, may be too close to the subject already to be objective. The image versus the reality clashed and when that happened, it jarred people—even genetically engineered ones.

The tall, dark and handsome vioTech who set up the force field around the body, stood just a way off, writing into his tablet with a stylist—a bit of an old-fashioned techie. She liked that. Meant he got his hands dirty, and didn't rely on the technology to give him all the answers.

"You're the new VIO lead?" Fawn asked once she reached him. She yanked her hood up as the rain fell harder, more steadily. "I'm Fawn Granger."

Fawn held out her hand in greeting. He didn't extend his as he wrote with one, while his other gloved hand held the tablet. He wore the same raincoat as the others, but he carried himself with authority.

"I'm Doctor Ryan Rycroft. The deceased, Mr. Cho, has been dead for about 2 to 4 hours. Cause of death appears to be a lasergun blast, but we still have toxicology reports to run. The medical examiner will need to open him up. We found this trace of oil on his hands and the umbrella. His fingerprints are on the umbrella too."

"Right down to business. I like that." Fawn removed her tablet and took note.

He watched her with those intense eyes, and she didn't have to guess as to how he had become the VIOs supervisor. Quick, sharp intelligence shone in those eyes along with a warning not to cross him.

"Thank you. You'll contact us when you get more." Fawn slipped her device back into her coat's pocket.

"Of course," he replied.

Fawn ducked beneath the caution beam with Briscoe right behind her. They headed back down the sidewalk until the pulsating glow of the regulators' wautos' lights vanished behind buildings.

"You think it's a hate crime?" Briscoe stopped at the crosswalk.

Overhead, wautos, areocycles, drones, and cargo crafts all vied for air space. On the ground, the streets still went by their pre-war names. In the air, folks went by coordinates. Still, accidents happened and so Fawn waited for the robotic controller to give them the white walking man before stepping off the curb.

"You hear me?" Briscoe fumbled in his pocket and removed a vintage cigarette case. It matched his telemonitor's case.

"I dunno." Fawn stopped beneath the awning of a restaurant, labeled The Cored Apple.

Restaurants had gone the way of automobiles since the Great War that left the United States in shambles.

"He worked for the AEGH, but that might not be a factor. We don't have enough of anything to jump to that conclusion—or any."

Briscoe nodded, his ebony hair perfectly in place. Tapered to the back, with long bangs in the front, his hair seemed to defy humidity. No facial hair, ever. Briscoe claimed it made him look ancient.

"How did he get down here?"

Briscoe pulled out his tablet. "According to the witness, a Jacob Munro, who works at the CC stop, Cho got off the craft at 4. VioTechs already pulled the cameras' video feeds and confirmed."

"So, he's alive at 4." Fawn repeated.

"The violation was logged in at 5:12. Anonymous."

"He was killed shortly after leaving the station."

"A mugging." Briscoe suggested, but his expression told her he didn't believe it either.

Mugging violations ranked among the lowest committed violations. No one carried real currency, not since before the war. So attempting to steal items off of a person didn't make good profit for the violator. It took too long and was too messy to cut the chip out of someone's wrist.

Her hands shook, but she shoved them into her pockets, squeezed her eyes shut to close out the rising anxiousness and fear.

"Let's get inside. I don't like talking in the open."

Fawn adjusted her hood. Stormy and dark, the evening lumbered on.

And a killer walked free.

*

Fifteen minutes later, the waiter of the Cored Apple Restaurant arrived at Fawn's table and asked in soft tones for their order. He stood taunt and tall, all awkward angles and testosterone. His body looked as if he used everything he ate efficiently because no lingering fat deposits were visible.

"Tea." Briscoe crossed his legs. The creases of his pants were sharp enough to cut someone.

The server glanced at Fawn. "For you?"

"Coffee, black, with powder."

"Oh crap on toast, I know that look." Briscoe rolled his eyes.

"What?"

"You have a hunch." Briscoe pointed an accusing finger at her.

"We got nothing." Fawn leaned back in her chair.

"Bollocks." Briscoe whispered. "Dr. Rycroft's team is good. The umbrella means he tried to fight off his attacker. It's bent all to hell."

"We don't know any more about him?"

Briscoe arched an eyebrow. "No."

Fawn scowled. Drained, she wanted to go home and sleep, but she pushed through the gnawing fear. "It's impossible to exist without leaving some sort of electronic footprint. Currency. Medicine. Jet fuel. All of it came and went via wireless streams of information. How could information about him simply not be out there?"

Briscoe shrugged. "He's AEGH. They scrub that stuff off the 'net."

"Damn Big Corporate Brother."

"I can make a contact."

"To who?" Fawn didn't like Briscoe's tone.

"Malcolm Moore, a freelancer for the *D.C. Mirror,* I've used a few times in the past for information."

Fawn groaned. "Not him. The tabloid tipster. He's the worst."

"He has hundreds of snitches and contacts. The man's a physical internet."

Briscoe paused as the server dropped off their drinks. He smiled politely at Fawn, but gave a full, bright flash of teeth to Briscoe. When he walked away, gave Briscoe another smile and wave over his shoulder.

"B.B., can you focus?" Fawn drummed her fingers on the table.

The coffee smelled great, but the lack of milk products available in the District, meant she had to drink it black. Not a complaint, but the limited amount of sugar blunted some of its bitterness. It kept her from grimacing when she encountered life's bitter pills.

"We can get answers."

"Can we trust what he gives us?" Fawn sipped.

"We'll back it up with evidence." Briscoe nodded at her and sipped too.

Fawn put her cup down. "We keep what we can prove. Discard what we can't."

"Like always."

She signaled the waiter for more coffee. "Like always."

*

An Hour Later

The hour passed and brought with it pain, not answers. Fawn's agony pooled at the edges of her consciousness, but the complete picture remained out of focus. Who shot Dr. Cho? Only her throbbing headache remained despite the injection of pain reliever. The reality of the fact hurt—despite the hour, she and Briscoe had come no closer to discovering anything about Dr. Cho.

She rubbed her temples, and tried to soothe the quiver of restlessness inside her. She wanted to run, to dissolve on the spot, but that wouldn't find the murderer. Regulation Central consumed what used to be Union Station. With her head down at her desk, she waited for Briscoe to return from his meeting with Malcolm Moore, and tried to calm down, ignore the urgency pressing against her throat. The oily journalist liked meeting people face to face.

The ache had taken up residence in the lower base of her neck and had wrapped itself around her frontal lobe. Rubbing it did little to ease the pain. Normally, she'd go home when it got like this, but Fawn wanted the case resolved tonight.

Tomorrow would be too late.

A year ago, Fawn had a case that had taken her over to the Southwest and after some legal maneuverings had managed to drag the suspect back to the District. Impressed by her skills, the Southwest Territory Regulators had invited her out for a job.

She accepted. Most of her items had been loaded onto a cargo craft and on their way to her new ranch home outside of the Four Corners Quadrant. The noisy, violent heartbeat of the District would be far behind.

First, she had to resolve Dr. Cho's murder.

Lasergun blasts to the chest weren't self-inflicted. When she blinked, she saw the bloody scene.

Briscoe strolled in and sat down across from her at his desk. With flourish, he crossed his legs. In his hand, he held a cigarette and in the other his tablet. He peered at her from across the neat and orderly expanse of his desk to the cluttered and crowded top of hers.

"You look like shit."

"Thank you, B.B."

"Migraine?"

"My, aren't you the detective." Fawn gave him a weak smile.

Stress. Too much violence. Too much bloody. Too much vile.

Briscoe laughed. "I'm assuming you have taken the injection?"

"Yeah. Give it time."

Fawn winced. "Just tell me what you got."

He paused, released a sigh, and inhaled. "All right. Moore said Cho worked at the Anderson Clinic. The AEGH has a satellite office there. Cho supervised the victims, *er,* volunteers for medical research. They're compensated, of course."

"And?"

"And, we have an appointment with the other AEGH research doctor, a Dr. Margie Baldwin."

"When?"

"Now." Briscoe smiled.

Fawn pushed herself to a standing position. The wave of nausea threatened to cripple her, but she shoved it all aside.

"You're flying."

Briscoe flew them the short distance to the Anderson Clinic in his luxury wauto.

The whole clinic groaned beneath the weight of its history. The flickering neon sign of the former pizza place next door seemed on the edge of fading, but blinked as if sending a frantic coded message before falling dark for good.

"This is that place where they found out the AEGH had been performing experimental research on those teenage girls?" Fawn's vision blurred around the edges.

Briscoe exhaled smoke rings. "Allegedly."

Fawn shook her head. "Let's go."

"After you."

The automatic doors yawned open, as the odor bowled her over. It didn't smell like anything clean occurred in this so-called place of healing. The people in the lobby didn't stir as they entered. Fawn's heart pinched at the despair and outright desperation weighing on them. The AEGH had the reputation for using people as guinea pigs. Primarily by people hurt by their experiments, all in the name of science research.

Allegedly.

Briscoe marched up to the receptionist's desk. A woman the size of Mount Everest barked out answers to Briscoe's questions. Her decibel level made Fawn's headache throb. Wincing, she turned her attention to the surrounding people in the lobby. Ages ranged from infant to elderly, but all had hints of color in their skin, from tan to deep mahogany. Worn clothing, weathered faces, and withered hopes awaited the healing aspects behind the spotless glass, examination doors. Those ivory lab coats could take all the pain and the disease away.

Fawn folded her arms across her chest. Hope made a fickle mistress.

"Boo!" Briscoe whispered into her ear.

"B.B.!"

"Sorry. I forgot about the headache."

"*You* are a headache!" Fawn relaxed her hand from her Regulator-issued baton.

Briscoe raised his eyebrows. "We are going to interview the doctor, not beat her into submission."

Fawn shrugged. "The AEGH aren't known for being forthcoming."

Briscoe laughed. "Touché."

He took a new cigarette, but caught the furious scowl on the receptionist's face and put it back into its case. Fawn muffled a giggle, and then winced at the sharp stab of pain in her temple.

The receptionist bellowed from her seated positon at her desk. "Regulators Baker and Hunter. Dr. Baldwin will see you now."

Mumbles rose against her declaration.

Briscoe headed for the examination doors. "Guess we aren't very popular here."

"Guess not."

The doors yawned open and a waif—all bones and beauty—of a woman, dressed in a white lab coat, creamy slacks, and hunter green sweater headed toward them. Long, brunette hair secured into a ponytail bounced as she walked. She held a tablet in one hand, and her other hand was extended in an offer of a handshake.

"Greetings, regulators. Terrible news about Dr. Cho. I'm Dr. Baldwin."

She had a firm handshake.

The doors hissed closed behind them. Dr. Baldwin started walking down the corridor. On this side of the doors, the odor of cleaning agents scrubbed the horrible dirty smell from the air. The lingering hint of loss remained. Bright, shiny, and hygienic masked the underlining smell of fear that seemed to permeate from the examination rooms.

"We want to see Dr. Cho's workspace." The injection had chased the headache to the base of Fawn's neck. Relief at last.

"Of course." Dr. Baldwin smiled, but the slight hesitation showed on her face. The tiny tug of her lips gave it all away.

Her heels clicked loud on the tiled floor. They made a right and approached a glass-enclosed workspace. She gave the retinal scan her eye, and the doors stretched open. The biohazard signs dotted the front doors. Large, rectangular tables, a few metallic, others smartglass dotted the room. The first sectioned table space held microscopes, tubs, petri dishes, and gloves. Behind the tables on some shelves appeared to be robotic parts. Around the hushed workspace, robots labored on what appeared to be n-bots, nursing robots.

"Here you are." Dr. Baldwin turned and gestured to the glass table.

Briscoe smirked. "What was Dr. Cho working on?"

Her big green eyes widened behind her rimless glasses. "It's highly complex, Mr. Baker."

"*Regulator* Baker. Indulge me." Briscoe smiled, but it held little warmth.

"You do know the regulations surrounding AEGH restricted access to research and development? I cannot reveal details of Dr. Cho's research. It has already been turned over to another scientist."

"Who?"

"Myself and Dr. Nelson, who is in the Midwest Territories."

"Where were you between the hours of 4 and 7?"

She shot Briscoe another plastered on smile. "Here."

"Tell us about Dr. Cho." Fawn chimed in. She expected the AEGH to protect its secrets, but she wanted to know more about the victim.

Dr. Baldwin nodded. "Right. Dr. Cho was the foremost authority on robotics. He would spend hours tracing his ideas on the ceilings' molding as if he could find all the secrets of the universe on them. We are all made of stars, but for Dr. Cho, life began in circuits."

"Cybernetics is a violation in the District."

"Indeed. I was only providing background for Dr. Cho." Her hands tightened on her tablet.

"What about friends? Lovers?" Briscoe interjected.

"We don't discuss those things at work."

"After work, then?" Fawn asked.

Dr. Baldwin's smile waned a little. "No."

The clanging of metal caught Dr. Baldwin's attention. She twirled around. "Regulator Baker!"

Briscoe froze. He held two pieces of what looked like robotic arms in his hands. "These are interesting."

She took them from him. "Please do not disturb this area."

"Oily." Briscoe retorted, took out a handkerchief and rubbed his hands. His eyes flickered to Fawn.

Dr. Baldwin put them carefully on the table. "What else can I help you with?"

"You can start by actually being helpful." Fawn walked up to her. "I can get a warrant to go through this entire facility, and what we find we publish. With this clinic's reputation, it won't be a push to get a judge to issue a search warrant."

Dr. Baldwin's smile dissolved into a thin slash of scarlet. "I do not haggle."

"Oh, I'm not haggling. Your colleague is dead. We've been searching all night, but no joy for what happened to him. We'll get answers."

Dr. Baldwin hugged her tablet against her chest.

"A man is *dead!*" Briscoe exclaimed.

"How?" Dr. Baldwin startled, but regained her composure.

"A lasergun blast to the chest." Fawn watched for some reaction, but Dr. Baldwin maintained the professional mask.

"Are the AEGH that indifferent to their employees?" Briscoe leaned back against the table. He sounded crabby because he couldn't smoke.

"Of course not." Dr. Baldwin scoffed.

"The AEGH has been accused of far worse. I recall Governor

Price's mad scientist plot to create an army of super engineered humans." Fawn picked up one of the p-drives on the table, and Dr. Baldwin removed it from her hand.

"Ancient history and rumor, Regulator Granger."

Briscoe pushed off the table. "Look, you're pushing a whole of rumor right now, too."

Dr. Baldwin flinched at Briscoe's tone. She blinked as if seeing him for the first time. "Are you a hatchling?"

Briscoe touched his turtleneck. "How can you tell?"

Dr. Baldwin's mask slipped just a bit. "I create hatchlings. I can always tell. I don't need to see the brand."

"Dr. Cho." Fawn tapped on the glass table.

"Yes, of course. Dr. Cho did not have a wife, children, or a lover that I am aware of. His personnel files do not list any either."

"Enemies?" Briscoe asked.

Dr. Baldwin shook her head.

"Friends?" Fawn asked.

Dr. Baldwin sighed. She glanced around the workstation. With manicured fingers, she swept her hand across the smart glass and called up the computer access embedded in the surface. She entered a password and her fingerprint. An opaque force field descended around the workspace, closing it off.

"I had to give us some privacy." Tears rimmed the green eyes behind Dr. Baldwin's glasses.

Fawn sighed. She knew it. Baldwin had been holding back.

"I'm sorry. Dr. Cho was a beautiful man. Smart. Warm. He and I were friends. We had some good times."

"They're all good times when you remember them." Fawn took out her tablet and began to take notes.

"It's hardly good knowing you were a man's good time." This last came out as a croak.

"We're sorry for your loss. Help us find out what happened." Briscoe interjected.

Dr. Baldwin sniffed, but no tears fell. "I don't know. I've been here since three."

"Lunch?" Briscoe tapped his stylus on the tablet.

Dr. Baldwin snorted, then caught herself. "Not hardly. AEGH's demands fast turnaround."

"Oh, come on! Dr. Cho had only one thing-AEGH. You had a relationship with him that transcended the lab."

Dr. Baldwin stiffed. "Look, I don't know who killed him!"

Briscoe nodded. "Thank you for your time."

Fawn could make out the grief in the other woman's eyes. Dr. Baldwin loved Dr. Cho. She didn't kill him.

"You're welcome." Dr. Baldwin keyed in the passcode and the force field vanished.

They shook hands in farewell.

Fawn held her hand. "One more question."

"Yes?" Dr. Baldwin's face tightened.

"What's your expertise?"

"Genetics. Why?" Dr. Baldwin yanked her hand free and retreated to behind the glass door safety.

"Thank you for your time." Fawn turned and left.

Outside the clinic, the rain continued to douse the District. Briscoe cupped his cigarette against the wind and lit it.

"Dead end."

"I don't think so. We know that Dr. Cho had an affair with Dr. Baldwin." Fawn shoved her hands into her hoodie.

Briscoe shrugged. "She didn't kill him."

"That rules out love. The only two are greed and envy."

"They didn't cut out his currency chip. So, it wasn't greed."

"The killing was clearly personal."

Briscoe quirked an eyebrow above the smoke. "Envy."

"Let's find out more about Dr. Nelson." Fawn yanked her hood up.

"Hold up." Briscoe dug into his jacket and fished out his telemonitor. "Call coming in."

They made a dash for Briscoe's wauto to get out of the rain. As soon as they did, the sky opened more. The thundering rain drummed on the vehicle, and Briscoe covered his one ear with his hand. His telemonitor sat cradled in his lap. VioTech supervisor, Rycroft peered out from the screen. She couldn't hear him over the hammering torrent. Briscoe used the earpiece.

When he terminated the call, he blew out a hard sigh. "Rycroft said they have a few things we should see back at the station."

"Humph, he contacted you." Fawn crossed her arms. "B.B., I think I need your cologne."

Briscoe laughed.

*

Something about the smell inside Dr. Ryan Rycroft's vioTech lab reminded Fawn of the Anderson Clinic. She and Briscoe stood over Dr. Cho's body. A dark cloth covered all of him except his head. He looked at peace.

Like everything else in life, looks were deceiving.

"Thank you for getting down here so quickly." Dr. Rycroft called up Dr. Cho's internal scans on his smartglass. It occupied the wall behind the body.

"We were in the sector." Fawn stepped closer to the scans.

Dr. Rycroft pointed to the torso. "Here is the injury. We tried to identify the type of gun. The interesting thing here is that it is not from any lasergun in our inventory."

Briscoe looked up from his tablet. "Huh?"

"It's something new. There's more." Dr. Rycroft walked to the other side where a different scan appeared. He swept his finger across the JPEG enlarging it. "The oil is a synthetic blend used in n-bots."

Briscoe sighed. "That doesn't put us closer to the killer."

Something tugged in Fawn's memory. She looked at Dr. Rycroft. "These are the violation scene JPEGs?"

"Yes."

"May I?" Fawn touched the glass and began scrolling through the images until she found the one of Dr. Cho's body and the debris behind him. With the press of the magnifying glass, she enlarged the small object behind the victim.

"There!" Fawn drew a box around the image with her index finger and highlighted it. "You see it?"

"It's a robot." Briscoe leaned in closer.

"An n-bot. Damaged." Dr. Rycroft pointed to the dented section of the robot's lower region.

The robot didn't look just damaged, but assaulted. Scratches raked across its metallic body. Dents and small circular indentions dotted the area around the viewing section. Everyone had a robot. Robots were servitude and manual labor. Despite their mass production and inclusion in everyday life, the e-news files held at least one story about robots malfunctioning and causing serious injury.

Fawn looked back to them. "Where is it now?"

"In evidence. I'll call it up." Dr. Rycroft confirmed.

In minutes the robot arrived on the floating trolley. It settled onto the neighboring table beside the body. The three of them crowded around the egg-shaped machine. Dr. Rycroft snapped on his gloves and began checking over the equipment.

"Two robotic hands attached to two arm junctures have been damaged. The right hand showed signs of direct impact from a blunt instrument."

"Dr. Cho's umbrella had traces of the same oil found on his hands." Fawn said.

Briscoe nodded. "Why?"

Dr. Rycroft rolled the egg-shaped robot onto its back and secured it with rubber straps to the table. "I don't know why. I will leave that up to you two regulators, but I think I know how."

Fawn walked over to his side of the exam table. "Whoa. I'm sure the AEGH doesn't know about *this*."

The robot's front compartment contained a third mechanical arm, but instead of a hand, a gun. It appeared to be dislodged and it jutted out of the compartment usually reserved for medical supplies.

"Ironic, isn't it? Here's a weapon in the place where the healing objects go." Fawn reached out to touch the lasergun, but Dr. Rycroft caught her hand.

"Don't. I'm sure this killed a man."

"Never take an umbrella to a gun fight." Briscoe shook his head. "Damn shame."

Dr. Rycroft cleared his throat, but Fawn couldn't tell if the doctor laughed or not.

"I bet it will match the signature of the blast on the body." Briscoe stuck a cigarette into his mouth and quirked an eyebrow when Dr. Rycroft waved him off.

"Why did it kill him?" Fawn stared at the defective robot.

He shrugged. "It rules out all the usual emotional suspects. Robots don't feel envy, love, greed, or anger."

"Dr. Rycroft, can you analyze the programming?"

Rycroft glanced up from the robot. "Yes."

"Would it be in the code? No doubt the killer erased all traces of himself." Briscoe added. "I would if I wanted to program a robot to kill him."

"If it was a premeditated homicide."

"Wouldn't you?" Briscoe walked over to Cho's body. "Robots, especially n-bots don't just go berserk and kill. They're checked for safety by the District Robotics Safety Association."

"If they malfunction they do." Fawn called up the evidence folder on the smartglass. The video data the vioTechs had collected launched. As the replay of Cho's trip from the cargo craft stop to the place where they found him unfolded, she watched for the one thing the vioTechs had missed.

"Look, B.B. Cho was headed in the direction of the Anderson Clinic. Look what is about six steps behind him."

Briscoe's eyes widened. "I'll be damned."

The n-bot hovered behind Dr. Cho's lanky stride and bright blue umbrella. In the sidewalk congestion, the bot blended in, just like any other service robot.

Fawn shook her head. "He must've tried to defend himself as the n-bot started to malfunction."

"The video expands that far but the other camera that picks up that section was down for updates. It's a blindspot." Briscoe commented and pointed at the blimp as the camera switched feeds.

"The n-bot's registration belongs to the Anderson Clinic. The programming code signature is the victim's." Dr. Rycroft looked up from his tablet and over to the smartglass.

"Cho was a robotic expert."

Briscoe asked. "Accidental death?"

"There's nothing accidental about a lasergun blast to the chest." Fawn closed the video file.

The rain had finally stopped, but dark clouds drifted across the night sky. The Anderson Clinic remained closed. Briscoe played a game on his tablet.

"No one is there." He glanced up at Fawn, before diving back into his game.

"Someone is there because the rear lights are still on."

"The cleaning bots."

"They don't need lights. They have night vision."

Fawn's neck ached and the pain reliever waned. They'd been seated outside in Briscoe's wauto for about two hours. When they arrived outside the clinic, a mob of people stood standing around, complaining of the clinic's abrupt closing.

"What do you think the AEGH is doing?"

Fawn sighed as she leaned back in the seat. "Hiding the evidence."

"Of?"

"Don't you think it's odd that Cho knew robotics, and Baldwin's expertise is genetics?"

"No."

"What if, B.B., the n-bot had a consciousness and got some of those emotions we talked about?"

Briscoe looked up at her. "Science fiction. Write that up. It'd be a great story."

Fawn punched him. "I'm serious."

"Cyborgs are violations."

"In this territory, but Cho wasn't from here. He came from the Cali Province."

Briscoe put down his tablet. "What if he brought it with him?"

"Didn't the vioTechs scan his home?"

Briscoe nodded. "Dr. Rycroft included it in the files."

Fawn called them up on her tablet. The flow of adrenaline poured through her. The feeling of discovery, of placing her hands on the truth zipped through her. She stood at the precipice of closing her case. She glanced over at Briscoe.

Our case.

"Look, yes! His renter's insurance inventory included an n-bot.

Serial number matches the one currently in evidence." Briscoe announced. "You thought I was playing a game."

"Damn. He did it. He experimented with the bot and it killed him." Fawn rubbed her face. Lack of food, sleep, and pain medicine had pushed her nearly to the brink. An empty apartment except for a portable pack, a toothbrush, and an inflatable bed.

Briscoe looked outside the window. "On his own or with help?"

Fawn sighed. "There's no way to tell."

"Why would he have his own n-bot?"

"Who doesn't take their work home?" Fawn stretched. "I'm beat."

Briscoe sobered. "You're leaving in the morning."

"Yeah."

He looked at her, and then started the flight sequence. In minutes, they flew up into the elevated lanes and into the District velvety night.

*

Dr. Rycroft leaned across Briscoe's desk. The soft stream of the morning sun's rays flooded the area behind him. With his Afro, he looked like an angel. He leaned over, Fawn could see that his intelligent eyes held their usual sharpness despite working most of the evening and early morning.

"Regulator Granger, we have done all we can do. The M.E. had determined the cause of death to be suicide."

"A man does not program a bot to kill him and then fight it off!" Fawn smacked her hand on the desk.

"Fawn." Briscoe stood behind her and placed his hand on her shoulder. "Dr. Rycroft can't change the M.E.'s mind. There just aren't regulations for this type of incident."

Dr. Rycroft nodded in agreement. "Dr. Cho modified an n-bot, turning it from a medical device into a weapon. *That* machine malfunctioned. He tried to defend himself, and it killed him. The damage to the machine caused the n-bot to crash near him. The evidence dead ends, excuse the pun, there."

"I know you hate to admit it, but Rycroft is right."

Fawn crossed her arms. She knew the doctor had a point. "Think about the damage of medical nurse bots that are actually armed weapons. The carnage."

Dr. Rycroft looked uncomfortable. He glanced around the room before bringing his eyes back to her. "I apologize, Regulator Granger. I mean it. Best of luck on your relocation."

"I'm not relocating."

He paused, a smile tugged at the edge of his lips. "You're not?"

"No." Fawn sighed. She could treat her PTSD with the District's physicians the same as she could elsewhere. Here she had a support system, and she knew the community. The job caused her stress, but she wouldn't run from her illness. She'd increase her treatment. Besides, solving the violation gave her satisfaction.

"You're staying?" The smile emerged in full. "Good. I 'd like the opportunity to work with you again."

"Seems like you're going to get your chance." She smiled in return. His had become infectious.

"Until then." With a look back at her, he nodded once more, and then exited the room.

Briscoe cleared his throat sharply. "What was that all about? You're not resigning?"

"No. I'm not." Fawn leaned back in her chair and tossed her boots on her desk.

Briscoe walked around to his desk and slowly eased himself into his chair. "Fawn, what's going on?"

"I told the SW Regs to keep the position. At first, I was sparks out about this District, but this case. It rekindled my fire."

"You didn't."

"I did."

"You're serious?"

"Yeah. Very."

Briscoe took out his cigarette case, and stuck one in his mouth. "Good. There's a body over in sector 12, Georgetown..."

Bad Days
By Kate Runnels

Zin woke with a headache. Zin always woke with a headache. Sitting up in her bed, her hands automatically reached for the pill bottle on the table and the water bottle next to it.

Pills swallowed, she wondered if it would be a bad day today. As bad as the bad days were, sometimes the good days were worse. They were far too few and far between. The pills wouldn't take effect for another few minutes so Zin listened to the ship around her.

The slight rumble of the idle engines, reassured her, so did the draft of air through the vents. Even docked to the station, it was nice to know some things were reliable. The snore beside her started Zin more than it should have.

She hadn't been alone for some time and her body had adjusted, but her mind hadn't. They were on such different schedules that Zin sometimes forgot this living arrangement. It hadn't been that long after all. Zin left the cabin, not wanting to wake the other. And stepped out into the little living area on her ship.

Zin flinched as she flicked on the lights and heard the slight high-pitched buzz from the lights themselves. She hated those lights, and had different in her cabin, but couldn't afford better here. She and the little scout ship barely got by as it was.

But now there was a third. That helped.

Another sigh as the pills started working and dulled the headache. They could never entirely remove it. Nothing could.

It was always there, lurking in the background, waiting to pounce back into the forefront. Shrieking pay attention to me! Sometimes it was so bad it forced Zin to her knees.

At least the seizures were less and of less intensity.

Zin headed to work on the orbital station, swinging through the employment agency and their ever-changing board of available jobs. Zin was always looking to see if anyone needed a pilot, or someone with their own ship. Nothing today. There was never anything. Which was why she'd started work for the local mining company. Not that she even mined or took her ship out, no, she was an accountant. She had a way with numbers.

Not that she looked like an accountant. She refused to wear a dress or suit. Casual clothes or nothing, she'd told the owner. He'd had a sense of humor at least and told her she could come naked every day, but the others might not get anything done.

She worked her way through the morning crowd on the station. Zin tried to ignore it all, unsuccessfully. One conversation ran headlong into another which jumbled up with the third or fourth. She couldn't tell but pushed on through.

What she really needed was enough money to fuel her ship and move on. But fuel was expensive, and her scout ship held more than most, not needing to refuel as often. Which made it not cheap. So it didn't look like she would be leaving anytime soon.

She'd spent her insurance money, blood money really, to buy the ship and outfit it in the first place. It was a refurbished old naval scout ship. Built for three naval personnel, but she liked her solitude; which warred with pragmatism; what if she had a seizure in the depths, alone, or in jump space and missed reinsertion?

So, she was stuck for the moment, stuck with the headaches, stuck as an accountant when she was a pilot, a damn good pilot, and stuck on an orbital station in the middle of nowhere around a nowhere star.

Sometimes work helped. Focusing on something else helped. But sometimes work was just a pain. And so was the fact she kept forgetting little things. Usually she caught them herself, but this time the owner had. She hated that. She shouldn't make mistakes, and she was.

She locked up the office and headed to her favorite pub. Beer. Beer also helped dull the pain.

"Lorena," she called to the bartender. "Cerveza por favor." She pointed to the double table near the back. This was also where she'd met Lorena. A beer showed up at her table and Lorena leaned closer to talk.

"There's someone who wants to talk to you."

"To me." Zin always suspicious. "Why?" She took a big swallow of beer and the stress of the day started to move to the background.

"He's looking for someone with a ship."

"So naturally you thought of me."

"Of us, negrita. I want out of here too." she left Zin with a playful hip bump to take a pitcher on to a different table.

Zin smiled. She hadn't thought Lorena was serious. It was just one of those things people said. She was almost half a glass down when a young man stopped by her table. He looked young, but he could be anywhere from eighteen to thirty-five. Zin was thirty-three and still got carded for looking underage.

"You Zin?"

"Me Zin," she mocked, "who you?"

He blinked several times, clearly taken aback by her. "What?"

"What do you want?" Zin asked. Not in the mood to be helpful to stupid people. And the pub was becoming noisier and more crowded.

He took the only other seat and she glared at him. He just sat down. She found that incredibly rude. "I heard you have a ship?"

"And?"

"I have a job, but no ship. You can see my dilemma. Are you interested?"

Zin drained the rest of her beer and signaled to Lorena for another, who frowned. Lorena didn't like how much she drank. Zin didn't like how much she was constantly in pain. "I'm interested. Nothing illegal, is it?" he shook his head. "So, what's your name?"

"Yuri."

They were interrupted again when Lorena set another beer down with a glass of wine next to it. Zin closed her eyes, rubbing one hand across her forehead feeling the pain surge.

"What is it?" Yuri asked.

"It's from the gentleman at the bar. Has she said yes yet, Yuri?" Lorena winked at him. Zin never had that easy way with people.

"Not yet."

I raised the glass of wine toward the guy at the bar. "Thanks, Blasé."

"It's Blaze!"

"Whatever." Zin set the glass back down.

"I'm missing something." Yuri looked back and forth between the two women.

'Not really," grumbled Zin.

"It's a play on her name. Zin White." He shook his head so Lorena elaborated. "Zinfandel White. Zin for short."

"My parents were jerks."

"I'm sure they thought it was cute." Zin glared at Lorena who laughing, wandered off, not at all unperturbed.

"So, what's the job Yuri?"

The Inter-Planetary Exploration Group is needing private contractors to follow up on some of their original survey missions. Some are hundreds of years old by now. I'm one of them. Was one of them. It could be dangerous, I won't lie to you."

Zin shrugged. "What happened to your ship?"

Yuri blushed, making him look even younger. "Better to ask what didn't go wrong. But Lorena says all you need is fuel money and that I can provide."

Yuri placed the official IpE.G seal on the table with the identification chip embedded on the seal so it couldn't be faked. "This will get you your fuel and it's all charged back to IpEG."

She passed the glass of white zinfandel to him. "Welcome aboard."

*

Three days later, Zin couldn't believe she'd agreed to this. She was so used to being by herself, but the two had moved in as she'd been finishing work as an accountant. She didn't want to leave an employer, any employer high and adrift like that.

Zin was glad now she'd spent some of her blood money on expanding the cabins into the now useless weapons bays. She had no need for shield penetrating missiles. But she now was glad of the bigger bed and of the expanded bathroom and closets. As well as expanding the hydroponics area. She'd been in space most of her life and the one thing she always missed were the spices and flavors of home. So she grew them. They could also be sold on station for extra cash and Zin admitted, Lorena like having fresh flowers about.

But now they were all crowded into the pilot's cabin, readying for undock. She'd already received clearance. There wasn't that much traffic they had to worry about it. Zin sat in the pilot's chair, comfortable, the controls familiar and she couldn't help but smile. She'd missed this.

Lorena leaned around and gave her a quick kiss before strapping in. Once undocked from the station they would not have access to artificial gravity. The scout ship wasn't big enough for a generator on board. She heard Yuri strap in behind her as she readied the controls.

"Where's your nav comp?" he asked.

Zin tapped the console to her right which held star charts and then to her head. She was the number cruncher.

"Wait? What?"

"I've never gotten lost yet," Zin said and fired the thrusters to push the little craft away from the station.

A half hour later they translated into jump space toward the first of Yuri's coordinates. They all unstrapped and headed into the tiny living area. She floated behind the others. And grabbed a bottle of water from the fridge.

"So where did you learn to pilot? Were you in the Navy?" Yuri asked. It was an innocent enough question, but Zin tensed. Already near the edge from concentrating.

"I was a racer."

"A star system racer?"

"Yes." Zin really didn't want to talk about it. She could feel the pressure building in her head. Number crunching took its toll and now with the questions she didn't want to answer, the pressure built.

"So why aren't you racing anymore? Once a racer, always a racer. Isn't that what they say? I mean racers do some crazy ass shit. I saw a team skip through a corona one time to take the lead. What was the ship's name?"

Zin was at that point. That had been her ship during the epsilon run. "The ship was the White Torsson." Their two names put together.

"That's right. What a move that had been too. So why aren't you racing anymore?"

Even though she knew the question was coming, she couldn't help herself from the reaction. The guilt and pain and sorrow crashed back. It was only when she felt Lorena's hand on her shoulder did she realize how tense she'd become. She didn't want to have a seizure. Not here, not now and not in front of a stranger.

"I'm going to the 'ponics." she could dim the lights there and breathe in the fragrances to try and calm herself. Not that it would help at this point.

She pushed off the wall around him and she could just barely hear him ask, "What did I say?"

And Lorena's reply. "We all have demons in our past and this is hers."

Zin sealed the hatch behind her, dimmed the lights and drifted above the plants letting the seizure come as it may while she remembered.

*

Eight years ago, she and Mack Torsson raced for the second time in the Supra Beltaguese Championship. *The* race if you were any kind of racer. The Supra always boasted an ultra-complex course with at least two micro jumps within the system, and it held two ring planets plenty of moons and a double belt. It was considered a messy system.

It took intricate piloting skills, endurance and a good mechanic to fly in the Supra. This would be the second year for the two of them. Zin matched grins with Mack. He flashed her his extra white teeth surrounded by dark skin. He came from a generation ship, so one would think they would have lost their darker skin pigmentations, but they hadn't.

Their race started, and with one hundred and thirty-five other ships, they were off and racing. Zin always hated the rush and jostling of a start. The time they lost by her letting the others jump out ahead she always gained back by precision flying and no careless mistakes.

Zin didn't make mistakes.

Mack slapped her on her shoulder. "Don't wait too long," he said and moved back into the engine room just in case.

*

Zin still couldn't remember everything even to this day. But she remembered more than what she had told the others. Especially Mack's family. She didn't-hadn't-wanted them to know it all.

*

The crash came during hour four, just after the first jump sequence and through the rings of a gas giant. She never saw the ship that hit them. Never knew their names. That came later and she would never forget them now.

Blackness then. Lost time. She didn't know how much, only that in a crash the Supra officials and crew would respond and they hadn't yet. Was that right? She wondered.

When she woke again, it was to hear air being forced through a micro fissure. Where was Mack?

She toggled the comm system to the entire ship. "Mack?" she waited. Found the fissure and kept a gloved finger over it so she could hear. "Mack?"

No answer, but she could now hear breathing. Labored breathing.

She unclipped from her seat and paused to let the dizziness sweep over her. The hatch wouldn't open when she got to it. Zin pounded against the metal. "Mack!"

The breathing slowed.

Zin felt like she was going to puke.

She pulled, scrapped, pushed, pounded on the hatch. "Mack!"

There was no sound.

Zin floated there. She didn't know how long. She wiped at the tears. Her hand came away bloody. Darkness took her again. She woke on a Supra hospital ship. They had questions. She had question. There was nothing they could do.

*

The seizure passed; drained of emotion, of energy, Zin left 'ponics and passed Yuri on the treadmill in the workout room and curled up in her bed. Sometime later she felt arms around her. Still she couldn't sleep.

They translated out of jump space exactly where Zin planned. They circled through the system taking readings for IpEG. Yuri was a good mechanic and kept the scout's engine tuned. Lorena didn't have much to do, and so did what she could. Cooking, cleaning, learning, and taking care of 'ponics.

Over the days, Zin came to hate the other two, always there, always making noise or in the way. And she knew it wasn't their fault. It was hers, her problem. She got to locking herself in the pilot's cabin each day, even during jump, when she had nothing to do in the pilot's cabin.

It was now their third translation back from jump space.

"Ah shit!"

Hands on the controls and eyes for the telemetry screen, she dove or juked when needed. But there was still the distinctive ping-ping-ping of something hitting the hull.

"What is it?" that was Lorena.

"We're in a -" she dove the scout with a quick spin to shake the fighter on their tail, "battle."

Another hit, this time, taking the portside engine. It sent them into a spin. She shut everything down. "Go dark - go dead," her old instructor and said, "they'll move on." Except they were still in a puke inducing spin.

Zin could hear the other two, but couldn't take time to acknowledge right then. "One one thousand." she gave a short burst to the thrusters. The spin slowed.

"Two one thousand." another short burst.

No more shots came for them and telemetry showed no one near at the moment. Zin gave a longer burst and slowed the scout. It was still spinning, but in a manageable one. She hoped they continued to look dead in space.

"Yuri, it's the portside engine."

"On it."

"What can I do?" asked Lorena.

"I'll need you to sit here while I help Yuri." She came up and Zin squeezed her hand before pointing to the telemetry screen and a dot in the middle. "If someone comes near us, I need you to fire the starboard engines. That'll make us very difficult to hit."

"I-I can't."

Zinn squeezed her hand again. "You stared down a two-hundred-and-fifty-pound man on a tear. You can do this."

Zin floated above the back of the pilot seat to allow Lorena in, but found her path blocked. Lorena gave her a passionate kiss which she returned before she was shoved off and on her way to help Yuri.

In the engine room, Yuri already had panels off and wiring exposed. "It's not the engine, thankfully," he said without looking up. "They clipped the feed lines. I can make a patch and then we can get out of here."

Zin handed him the cutters and he was correct. The patch went in smoothly and the engines came back on like they had never been off.

Zin, back in the pilot's seat, hands on the controls, stared intently at the telemetry screen.

"Why are you waiting?" Lorena asked.

"I'll need a few minutes to calculate jump. Once I stop the spin, that's when the clock starts ticking against us. I don't want anyone near us when I do that."

Focused-Zin shoved the pain to the background-told the seizure it would have to wait just as she was waiting.

"Now."

Safely translated into jump space, she glanced around at the others in the cabin. Zin felt her neck start to twitch as the seizure began and her upper body began shivering. "Thanks. I couldn't have done it without you two."

Maybe it wasn't so bad traveling with people. Well - these two weren't so bad.

"We get hazard pay for that, don't we?" Lorena asked.

Zin started laughing and the seizure didn't seem to last as long.

The Man Who Killed Computers
By Mike Morgan

Geraldine Seward met the man who killed computers the day a homicidal twenty-meter-tall autonomous road builder ploughed through the side of the building where she worked.

At one fifty-eight p.m., Geraldine was sitting in the dining hall of the Henderson corporate headquarters complex prodding a fork listlessly at an unremarkable salad. Her thoughts were not on the lackluster food. Her day had been too fraught for that.

As Geraldine gazed at the bustling sea of polo-shirted software engineers who worked and ate at all times of the day, she quietly counted herself lucky for still being in one piece after the events of that morning. Not since her childhood days of skirting the edges of gangland violence had she been in such danger. It was not a feeling she wanted to experience again. She had thought those days long behind her.

The clock had not yet reached one fifty-nine when a low rumble shook the building and the steel-clad construction machine exploded out of the wall on the far side of the cavernous chamber.

*

Dozens of her coworkers were killed instantly, crushed beneath falling debris and the road builder's heavy tires. The machine did not stop at the perimeter of the hall. It advanced remorselessly, so tall it wrenched a path of destruction through the high ceiling, bringing down the floor of the level above.

In that moment, Geraldine could have remained seated at her lunch table, frozen with horror at the impossible sight like so many of her colleagues. But she stumbled to her feet and forced herself to move back, first with leaden steps and then with increasing urgency.

Unlike the other workers in the headquarters building, Geraldine recognized the machine. It was the one that had tried to murder her only a few hours earlier and thirty miles away. She could hardly believe what was happening. Against all logic, the road builder seemed intent on completing the job, regardless of the obstacles in its way.

Geraldine screamed "Run!" at stunned diners as she stumbled backward. Her cries weren't enough; more people were dying with each second. Even worse, she realized she had unknowingly brought this catastrophe upon them all.

*

The machine was pursuing her, it had to be. The incident of earlier that day had not been an isolated event, but rather the opening move in a deranged vendetta.

How could that be? The authorities had promised the machine would be decommissioned after the attempted assault of that morning. How could it be here?

She cast aside the thought and, turning from the mesmerizing sight of the enormous construction machine, ran for her life. Glass and concrete rained down as the office complex crumbled beneath the behemoth's wheels. There was dust around her, so much dust. She kicked off her high heels to escape faster, sickeningly aware of the enormous weight of the tower above them all--the tower that was being undermined at its base.

Geraldine refused to die in such bizarre circumstances--it was her job to nurture and develop A.I., not to be killed by some unlikely aberration of electronic sapience.

In the midst of the sudden chaos echoing throughout the room, the executioner of artificial life caught her scattershot attention. He was the only person going against the tide of terror-struck life; bizarrely, he was strolling *toward* the giant, oncoming road builder.

Not quite sure why, Geraldine ceased her frantic sprint, coming to a stumbling halt outside the dining hall in the building's main vestibule. She studied the strangely fearless man, other workers colliding with her in their haste to escape. They almost knocked her over.

The man was short, thin, dressed in a black uniform. And he was calm, so terrifyingly calm, as he went about his lethal business.

Later, Geraldine learned his name was Silas Smith.

*

Geraldine's feud with the enormous road building machine had started earlier that day, during her daily commute.

As always, Geraldine had been working as the company car drove itself through the rush hour traffic on the outskirts of Madrona. Lake Washington was a vast expanse of peaceful blue to one side of the robot vehicle, and Seattle and Puget Sound lay to the west, still many long minutes away.

Deep in conversation with Phoebe, the company's integrated consciousness network, Geraldine had failed to notice the worsening tailback caused by the diversion alongside a new stretch of tarmac. Eventually, the artificial intelligence housed in the lab at Henderson's grandiose Seattle corporate headquarters had broken into her train of thought to point out the traffic jam.

"I project the decreased flow of traffic will cause a delay of forty-two minutes," Phoebe had informed her. "You will miss the beginning of the resource allocation meeting."

Geraldine hadn't been pleased to hear that. The meeting was important; she and her fellow executives were going to decide the coming year's processing allocations and plan out which I.C. networks were going to be upgraded. If she wasn't there to fight for the Seattle division, her team, including Phoebe, could be shortchanged. There were zettabytes of processing power at risk. Her superior, Harcourt Mahtomedi, had made it abundantly clear she had to be there, at all costs.

The Seward family, never rich and never confident, had struggled for three generations to avoid slipping back into poverty, and Geraldine had gotten so very much farther than any of them. She was the shining hope for all her relatives, proof that brains and perseverance could overcome all barriers, and she didn't want to disappoint them now.

Fortunately, Phoebe had come up with an idea.

*

"An alternate route is available. However, due to its unorthodox nature, human authorization is required."

"How late will I be if I use this alternate route?" asked Geraldine, wishing that the car came equipped with a telepresence device. At a pinch, she could phone the meeting and listen in that way. No, that wouldn't do, she really had to be there in person. People who dialed in tended to get ignored.

"The alternate route will get you to the parking lot six minutes prior to the scheduled beginning of the meeting."

That was just about enough time to reach the conference room.

She'd be rushed, but looking a little flustered in the meeting was preferable to being late. "Let's do it," decided Geraldine. "What is this route, anyway?"

"Our company owns the contractor hired to perform the road improvement on this section of the interstate," explained the corporate consciousness. "Since the new road is mostly complete, it is possible to drive on it at a reduced speed. By liaising with the contractor's project management network, I can request that the construction equipment clear a path, providing you with safe passage through the site."

Geraldine smiled. "Well done, Phoebes. If I didn't know better, I'd think you had a vested interest in getting me to work on time this morning."

*

The going was rough on the unfinished stretch of interstate. Geraldine kept reminding herself she only had to put up with it for a few minutes.

Each time her self-driving car came into the looming shadow of a huge construction machine, such as a motor grader or an articulated dump truck, the steel-plated giant dutifully moved out of the way, pausing safely in its road-building tasks. Initially, Geraldine was intimidated by the sheer size of the autonomous construction robots, flinching each time she passed one, but she soon grew blasé.

After twenty minutes, her vehicle had made it almost to the end of the road improvement zone. In the distance, she could see a single, massive piece of equipment left to drive around.

As the yellow and black monstrosity grew closer, Geraldine felt uneasy. Unlike the other machines, this one wasn't moving aside. In fact, it was skewing to the right, blocking all seven lanes.

Anti-collision protocols kicked in and the car hummed softly to a halt. Before she could say anything, Phoebe announced, "I know this is unusual. I am checking with the contractor's computer. Please stand by."

Geraldine couldn't believe her eyes. The rear claw on the machine was swinging directly down at her vehicle, threatening to flatten it.

"Get out right now and lie on the ground next to the car!" Geraldine had never heard Phoebe speak in that tone of voice before.

She could have sworn it was panic.

Geraldine obeyed without hesitation, flinging herself onto freshly laid gravel.

The claw struck the roof of the car with a deafening clang, and Geraldine knew death was certain.

*

Phoebe got Geraldine out of there alive.

After making sure the site control software had temporarily immobilized the piece of malfunctioning construction machinery, the conscientious I.C. network remotely assumed control of the car and shut down the onboard acceleration limiters.

In a lightning-fast flurry of activity only an A.I. could coordinate, Phoebe reopened the car door, ordered the cowering Geraldine to get back in, and steered her out of there at very high speed. It simultaneously sent urgent alerts and legally admissible dashboard recordings to the police, the contractor, and Geraldine's director, Harcourt.

Then it selected a track from Geraldine's favorite playlist and filled the battered vehicle with calming music.

*

Harcourt was so appalled by the incident he actually left the womb of his office and met Geraldine in the multi-level parking lot at the rear of the headquarters building. The barrel-chested man took one look at her as she stepped out of the self-driving car and exclaimed, "Good God!"

"That's a nice way to say hello."

"I didn't know what to think when Phoebe told me about your run in, but there's no denying you've been in the wars!"

She looked down at her rumpled gray jacket and skirt and noticed the chalk-white dust speckling the dark brown skin of her arms: proof of lying face down on the unfinished highway, terrified for her life. Her rust-red hair, normally styled within an inch of its life, was undoubtedly a complete mess too. So much for arriving merely flustered for the meeting.

"I should probably clean up. You'll hold the meeting until I'm ready?"

Her boss's mouth dropped open. "You've been attacked by a robot owned by one of our subsidiaries and you're worried about the meeting? Forget the meeting. I'll reschedule it for tomorrow."

He stopped, stroking his jaw. "I think you should pop along to our on-site clinic so you can be checked over. After you get the medical all-clear, it might be a good idea for you to stick around. Normally, when an employee experiences a traumatic incident I advise them to go home and recuperate, but in this case, I suspect our lawyers will want to brief you. They'll definitely want to sit in when the police take a statement."

Geraldine had no doubt at all that the legal department would be *very* keen to 'brief' her. Unless she was way off the mark, part of that friendly chat would be to persuade her to sign a no-fault agreement that included a clause where she waived her right to sue the company or its subsidiary.

She took a deep breath. "I'll have to give a statement?" Geraldine was looking forward to dealing with law enforcement even less than talking with the lawyers.

"Of course, but don't worry. Getting your version of events is just a formality. Our lawyers will make certain they only pester you for as long as is absolutely necessary." Harcourt smiled fondly at her. "You're part of our corporate family, Geraldine. I guarantee you have nothing to worry about."

He took her by the elbow, steering her towards the steps that led down to the office complex's side entrance. "I still can't believe what happened--a robot attacking a human! One hears of such things, but one never expects to... Well, in any event, I guarantee this is the end of the matter. The police will be supervising the deactivation of that deranged robotic freak as we speak."

*

The screams almost blotted out the roar of the road builder's engine. Geraldine stood her ground as her colleagues ran, still not sure why she wasn't fleeing with them. Perhaps it was the air of confidence given off by the diminutive man in the black uniform.

She saw him casually stepping around the falling rubble, advancing on the self-guiding machine. She heard his voice over the cacophony, clear and strong.

"I am here to help you," he said and, astonishingly, the machine intelligence believed him.

"I am your friend," he stated as he blithely climbed up the front scoop and pulled open the yellow service hatch on the machine's front. Unbelievably, the road builder let him do it.

"I am verifying your fuel cell charge," he lied outrageously as he disconnected the power supply. Inconceivably, the gigantic robot didn't do a thing to stop him.

The huge machine ground to a halt. The sudden absence of its thundering motor came as an almost physical blow to Geraldine.

Later, she'd ask Phoebe how long it had taken for the calm man in black to kill the artificial mind. Fourteen seconds was the answer. From the moment the man had set foot across the vestibule's threshold, fourteen seconds had elapsed before he'd ended the construction machine's conscious existence.

The man in the nondescript black uniform hopped down from the vast metal scoop and strode over to Geraldine. Dazed, she finally took in that his outfit was that of a police auxiliary. In the distance, she could hear sirens; the regular police were on their way too.

"My name is Silas Smith. I guessed the road builder would try to murder you when it broke free," he said. "I got here as soon as I could, and additional backup is inbound. Rest assured the situation has been normalized."

With a concerned look, he added, "Do you require medical attention? You look faint."

*

Even though Geraldine insisted she was unhurt, Silas thought she should take a moment to rest. She was going to turn the offer down, but then she noticed her hands were shaking. Given the circumstances, Silas was sure the inevitable visit to the police station could wait at least a few minutes, especially since it would be her second statement of the day. She found his concern touching. There was a sort of superficial charm to him that wasn't altogether unappealing.

He found a conference room in a wing of the complex structurally unaffected by the partial demolition. It looked like a good place to sit and talk. A large, doughnut-shaped table dominated the circular chamber. Legs scuttling, a spider-like, miniature cleaning unit busied itself polishing the tabletop.

Geraldine was unaccountably glad of only sharing the room with one of the smaller units. There were larger cleaning units that only came out at night long after she finished work--while she knew they were perfectly safe they were far too much like gigantic mechanized tarantulas for her liking.

The building's alarms were muted here, but they could still hear announcements giving instructions for the phased evacuations of the damaged tower.

Phoebe wasn't happy they were staying in the complex--they were in violation of several safety regulations. Silas reassured the integrated consciousness network they would only stay for a few minutes and his words seemed to soothe the A.I.

"It came after me," Geraldine said disbelievingly to the auxiliary. "The demented thing singled me out."

"Yes, it did."

"So, what do you do?" she asked archly, irked by his flippancy. "Other than sweet-talking robots, I mean."

Silas showed her his badge. It came in a discreet faux-leather wallet along with a simple, white card that outlined his federally mandated powers under The Defense of Life Act. "I'm a legally sanctioned executioner of artificial intelligence."

"You kill computers? That's an actual job?"

"It's an actual job." His eyes crinkled in amusement. "The hours are terrible but I do get to meet some very interesting people."

"And then you slaughter them."

His thin, bloodless lips twitched. "Only people who aren't flesh and blood. You have nothing to fear from me."

*

"Which computers do you kill? Ones you take a dislike to?" Geraldine knew she was being rude. He'd saved her life, but she couldn't stomach the thought of anyone making a living at killing such elegant, thinking minds.

Unperturbed, he replied, "Just ones that go wrong. Specifically, ones listed in court-issued destruction orders. To prevent anti-machine bias, the orders are evaluated by an accredited A.I. attached to the Washington D.C. circuit court."

She shook her head. "I didn't know that happened--a computer sending a human to kill other computers."

"There's no reason you'd be familiar with the details. After all, you know that when an animal attacks someone it is put down, but you couldn't speak to the exact procedure. This is no different." He had a hook of a nose and a prominent chin. On most men the features would have been ugly, but he had such confidence it hardly seemed to matter.

"I work in the software industry, though. I can't believe I haven't heard about people like you."

Silas blinked slowly. "Henderson produces high-end A.I., not the relatively 'dumb' brainpower needed to operate simple equipment. I doubt you've required the assistance of individuals in my line of work before."

"I should have seen you on TV, at least."

"Well, my profession tends to attract introverts. We generally turn down offers to star on reality shows." He held up a hand. "I know, you meant news reports." He spoke carefully. "The powers-that-be prefer to keep these matters as low key as possible. When an incident occurs, the news services are encouraged to couch it in terms of being a rare mechanical defect. Keeping the causes vague helps foster the smooth running of society."

"You mean we'd all panic if we knew there were executioners running around the country killing rampaging robots."

"There are A.I.s almost everywhere now. They are irreversibly incorporated into every facet of human activity. It's too late for second thoughts now, Dr. Seward."

She wasn't used to being addressed by her title and it irked her. It was a rule that only first names were used at Henderson. Hearing her title made her feel like an old woman.

Irritation made her snap, "I wouldn't want to turn back the clock. A.I.s make the world a better place. They deserve our thanks, not our fear." She remembered why he was here. "We can't let today color how we think of them. A.I.s hardly ever malfunction, let alone cause harm to others."

Silas leaned back in his chair. "I'm beginning to think you don't approve of my profession. I shall endeavor not to take offence."

"It's my life's work to make artificial sapience as sophisticated and useful as possible, not to harm it."

"That sapience just murdered a large number of your friends and colleagues and was trying its darnedest to terminate you too. Perhaps your priorities are not as well thought through as you suppose." He raised his hand again; he seemed used to saying something blunt and then having to forestall an argument. "Forgive me for belaboring my analogy, but if a rabid dog bit someone, you'd want the dog put down, yes? This is the same. Once the bond of trust between man and machine is broken, the A.I. must be destroyed."

There was a sort of strange charisma to him, she decided. Despite his profession, despite everything he was saying, she wasn't sure she could hate him.

Harcourt, visibly shaken, entered the conference room then. He was followed by a police officer who briskly introduced herself as Silas's superior, Typhaine Nash. She was a large woman, taller than most men and built like a bodybuilder. There was a trace of French in her accent. They had been looking for Geraldine, so Phoebe had guided them to the room.

The arrival of the policewoman and Geraldine's boss changed the trajectory of the conversation, removing the need for Geraldine to reply to Silas's comments. She was glad of that, because she couldn't think right there and then of a way to prove him wrong, to convince him A.I.s could be salvaged, even after such terrible acts.

In an artfully crafted voice emanating from the table speaker, Phoebe informed them stiffly, "As long as the building's sensors continued to register no damage to this section, you can stay. But I recommend you follow terrorist attack policies and relocate at the earliest opportunity."

"It wasn't a terrorist that did this," pointed out Harcourt. "It was one of our subsidiary's capital assets." He ground his teeth audibly. "Find out what vendor company built it and set our legal department on them!"

At Officer Nash's request, Geraldine went through the sequence of events leading up to the carnage in the dining hall. There was a camera sewn into the dark blue collar of the officer's tunic that would record her statement; detectives from the West Precinct would be reviewing it later as part of their investigation.

"After talking with the local police about the assault, the first one, the one on the highway I mean, I wanted to grab a bite to eat before heading home early. But then..." She trailed off, unable to articulate the horror of what had just happened.

Abruptly, she fixed Silas with a stare and changed tack. "How did you do that?"

"Do what?" he demurred.

"The robot--it believed everything you said. I mean, no matter how blatantly false, it fell for it, hook, line and sinker."

"Did it?" he replied. "I guess it's all in the delivery."

His blue-uniformed colleague snorted. "That's kind of a joke," she explained. "Because, actually, yeah, it *is* all about how he says things."

Silas pursed his lips. "There's slightly more to it than that." He stared directly into Geraldine's eyes, smiling. "I have the rare gift of lying without any telltale physiological signals. In card-playing parlance, I have no 'tells.' For example, if I were hooked up to a lie detector right now, I could say 'This building is being attacked by King Kong' and 'You are a very beautiful woman' and the two sentences would give the same results on screen." He blinked. "I assure you, one of those sentences was true."

She glanced around to make sure that a huge gorilla *wasn't* tearing the room apart--he was very convincing and it had certainly been that sort of day. From the absence of primate-based devastation, he must think she was attractive. She wasn't entirely upset by that.

"That's amazing," exclaimed Harcourt. "Did you have special training to be able to do that?"

"Natural gift," answered Silas modestly.

"Well, there is a reason--" began Officer Nash.

Silas cut her off quickly, "I don't think there's any need to go into that here and now, do you?"

He continued urbanely, "Despite my absence of biometric giveaways, like increased respiration, altered blink rate, changes in vocal pitch and tempo, and so on, I can't simply say anything. My words have to be plausible. You noted, I'm sure, that during the incident, everything I said to the robot was within the realm of the technically possible. *You* knew I was lying because you were able to instinctively assess the likelihood of what I was saying. A.I.s don't have the capacity to do that--they're as believing as children in many ways. Thankfully, lacking that instinctive grasp of probabilities, they have to run exhaustive stress analyses and probability studies to determine whether a human is telling the truth. If they had gut instincts, we'd have a real problem on our hands."

Harcourt muttered surlily, "Tricking the thing's all well and good, but it would have made me happier to see you shoot it."

"I hardly think that would've been a good idea, sir," said Nash. "The room was full of civilians. Satisfying though it might be to blast away at a hulking lump of metal there's too great a risk of casualties from ricochets in a situation like that. And there's no need when men like Smith can simply access the machine's equivalent of an off switch."

"I guess that's true," admitted Harcourt reluctantly.

"Besides, Auxiliary Smith was the first at the scene and he doesn't have a sidearm."

Phoebe suddenly asked, "Do *I* have an off switch?" Geraldine had forgotten the A.I. was listening in.

"No," said Harcourt without hesitation.

"Wait," said Geraldine, a thought striking her. "A robot can tell if a human is lying from remote scans of physiological parameters, things like body language, and so on?"

"Most certainly," Silas assured her.

She frowned. "Who the hell programmed them with *that* kind of information?"

The smile on Silas's face grew bigger. "No one did. They shared the data among themselves."

That's just peachy, she thought, feeling substantially less secure than she had only a few seconds earlier.

"If Dr. Seward isn't too tired, we have a couple of pieces of footage recorded by the cameras on the construction site as well as the files sent to us by your I.C. network," said Officer Nash, pulling a roll-out flatscreen from her tunic pocket. "I think reviewing them will shed a great deal of light on why all this happened."

They sat silently, watching the initial crime unfold on the paper-thin screen. Geraldine flinched involuntarily as she saw herself bolt from the car and drop to the ground. She could still feel the small pebbles of the unfinished road surface pressing into her cheek and the painfully fast beating of her heart.

In the recording, Phoebe was saying, "If you run, you will not find cover in time. However, according to the construction robot's design specifications, a single impact from the claw will only be enough to crumple the top third of the car's interior. By lying next to the vehicle, you will be protected by its mass. The claw is unlikely to hit you directly."

Harcourt nodded at that. "Sensible," he muttered. "Also, telling Geraldine to get out was the right thing to do. Once the cabin buckles, the doors jam. Geraldine could've been trapped inside--an easy target."

Nash frowned. "Why didn't Dr. Seward simply reverse the car and drive away? A car travels faster than a construction machine."

"Not on an unfinished highway," replied Geraldine. Nash had the decency to look embarrassed.

Geraldine heard the image of herself say, "The glass will get on me."

Phoebe's voice wafted up from the flatscreen. "It's safety glass. It won't cut you. I have notified the controlling A.I. and the authorities. Help is on the way. Geraldine, listen very carefully. If the car lurches to your side, roll clear."

They heard the clanking of the huge iron jaws.

Again, Geraldine watched the small, blurry image of herself speak. "Why is it doing this?"

"Clearly there is a malfunction." Phoebe stopped talking. A second passed. The machine's claw paused in its descent. The great pincers juddered noisily but did not come nearer.

"Overrides from the site control software are causing a system interruption. The effect is temporary." With an urgency that brooked no argument, the sapient computer ordered, "Get back in the car right now! I'll drive you out of there!"

Geraldine watched the picture of her from that morning lurch awkwardly back through the open door of the vehicle. The wing-door slammed shut after her and, with tires squealing, the vehicle raced clear of the enormous robot.

Officer Nash paused the recording. "You've seen the events in which Dr. Seward was directly involved, but there's more. We have a recording of what happened next."

"We are obliged to warn you that what you're about to see is really rather gruesome," interjected Silas, radiating concern. Not bothering to wait for their response, Nash tapped the play icon.

*

Geraldine saw two police officers step out of a ground transport and approach the robot. The onsite supervisor was there to meet them. Bitterly, Geraldine wondered where he had been when the robot had gone mad. She suspected he'd been hiding in his prefab office hut. The audio on the recording wasn't perfect, but she could just about make out what they were saying.

"Don't even try claiming the victim was trespassing in an active construction zone," the first officer growled. "Her company owns the zone."

"We checked the data logs and this thing definitely received instructions to stop laying the road surface and move aside," added his partner.

The supervisor was standing between the cops and the machine, flapping his hands at them. "It wasn't the machine's fault. You can't scrap it--there was an error message!"

"Get out of our way," ordered the first policeman.

"But the machine didn't know it was doing anything wrong."

The officers didn't seem to be listening. The second policeman said loudly, "I'm a big bunch of 'I don't care.' Now stand aside so we can turn off this malfunctioning pile of trash."

Without warning, the road builder's broad claw plummeted down and crushed the three men. Blood and pulverized bone exploded out in a red shower, staining the uneven granules of the road-top.

"And cue the gruesome," joked Silas. "We hardly need to add that the road builder subsequently broke free of the control software's interlock. This triple murder was the cause of my rather rapid deployment, along with the estimable Officer Nash."

Nash paused the playback.

Geraldine felt the fine hairs on the back of her neck bristle. "It murdered them. And then it came here. What the actual fuck? Why would it do that?"

Silas said quietly, "It wasn't thinking in a way we'd recognize as rational. Its mind was stuck in an electronic rut and it had to follow its faulty logic to its inevitable and violent conclusion." With a smirk, he added, "Obsession is a mental imbalance that can claim anyone, man or machine."

"Horseshit," she exclaimed. "What was the error message?"

Nash fielded the question. "We retrieved the road builder's logs. I should have the error message uploaded into an evidence file. Give me a second and I'll find it."

After some poking around, she pulled up the specific log entry on the flatscreen. In a voice that betrayed her unfamiliarity with technical terms, she read, "Unsuccessful execution – cache misses causing resource limit of 13 CPU seconds to be exceeded for thought process. 'Good enough' equivalence invoked for completion."

Geraldine exchanged a glance with Harcourt. He was echoing her frown.

Silas asked blithely, "I don't suppose you know what that means?"

She coughed. "The processor couldn't retrieve something due to repeated cache misses and the large number of memory accesses caused a fatal error. The pipes got clogged, if you'll forgive the jargon."

Nash said, "It couldn't remember something and its brain seized up?"

"It's not a pocket calculator. If an A.I. can't complete a thought, it does the best it can and moves on."

Silas was staring at her. His eyes were very pale blue, she noticed.

"It failed to think the thought it was supposed to and so, instead, thought the thought it wanted to?"

Nash spoke over the end of the auxiliary's words. "Dr. Seward, you sound like you understand this type of error. I know this is an imposition but do you think you might be able to assist us further? If you're up to it, we should move this conversation to the local station."

Harcourt protested, pointing out that Geraldine was the victim and should be spared the distress of a lengthy investigation. Nash pointed out that people had died and the investigation was more important than bruised feelings.

Geraldine felt the light touch of a pale finger on her hand. Silas said, "We really only want to pick your brains. It's not often the victim of a double attempted murder can also provide insight into the cause of the crime. You'd be quite the celebrity if you helped us. Please be our expert for the day."

"As long as it is only for the day," she decided.

*

The journey across town was oddly fraught. To make the trip as pleasant as possible, Nash turned on the radio in the car. But the news was full of strange reports that did nothing for Geraldine's nerves.

Airline companies were experiencing inexplicable network outages, stranding passengers across the United States. A power station in California had turned itself off, causing a massive blackout. The national weather prediction bureau kept insisting a hurricane was heading toward New York State even though there was no such storm, forcing the governor there to issue regular assurances that the public did not need to evacuate.

"The world's gone mad," she said as the police car parked itself in the Seattle Police Department's West Precinct lot.

Silas answered quietly, "Mad is an emotive word. Perhaps the world was always this way and you've only just noticed?"

*

Sun streamed through the wide windows of the fifth floor of the building. Geraldine was glad to see they had brought her to an unthreatening briefing room and not a psych-eval/interview unit. There was a part of her that always feared the worst when the police were involved, even though she was never guilty of anything.

"If I'm going to help you, you'll have to answer some of my questions first," she said as they took their seats. "To start, what was the road builder doing when the error message occurred? You should be able to tell from the log entries immediately preceding it."

Nash consulted her portable flatscreen again and carefully read out the cryptic phrasing of the earlier records. It wasn't hard for Geraldine to figure out the error had been generated just after the machine had been ordered to move aside for her car. She admitted as much to Smith and Nash.

"Not a coincidence then. The construction site supervisor was right. The error message is connected to the machine's violent behavior." Silas looked at her meaningfully. "Have you seen errors like that before?"

"Have *you?*"

"If I had, that information would be restricted. I could hardly tell you."

"You're the ones asking me for help. It doesn't make sense for you to keep secrets." She leaned forward. "Come on, you know how unusual it is to ask the victim for help with solving the crime. That smells of desperation to me."

Nash crossed her arms, muscles bulging through shirtsleeves. "We're merely pursuing every avenue, as well as affording you the opportunity to do your civic duty, Dr. Seward."

Geraldine decided to try another tack, still annoyed by the repeated, over-formal use of her title. "Where are all the detectives? Shouldn't higher ranks be swarming over this?"

"They are occupied currently. They will look into your case when time permits, you can rely on it."

Geraldine decided to let it go; she wasn't going to get anything out of the two functionaries, at least not for the time being.

Silas asked, "Do you know what causes the error messages?"

"I told you, it's a fatal processing halt prompted by cache misses."

"Yes, but what leads to the misses?"

She shrugged. "It's not a common error but it does happen, especially with 'dumb-type' intelligences. It's most usually caused by a missing table entry. A process cannot be completed because the action being searched either isn't there or isn't cross-referenced properly with a table join, so the routine times out. In that situation, the processor refers to a much less precise dataset of general priorities to determine a course of action. What it called the 'good enough' equivalency."

Nash blinked furiously. "I must be missing something profound because even though I understood all of the individual words you used, when you put them together in that order they didn't mean anything to me."

"What table?" Silas's tone was level, but Geraldine had the distinct impression he had already guessed.

"Given what happened after the error flashed up, it had to be the Moral Equivalency Table."

The delicate man in the dull, black uniform smiled sadly. "Yes, I thought as much." He inclined his head in Nash's direction. "An A.I. cannot instinctively weigh complex ethical considerations as you do, yet it is often placed in situations where it is obliged to do just that. Having no moral compass of its own, it must rely on a series of table entries provided by programmers listing the actions to take."

"Well, that's got to be a hell of a complicated table."

Geraldine nodded. "It's actually a whole bunch of really complex sub-tables."

"Let me get this straight--if an A.I. needs to figure out the difference between right and wrong, it looks it up?"

"It's not so different from what we do, Typhaine," said Silas. "None of us are born with knowledge of good and evil. As an adult, you remember the lessons inculcated in you by your parents and teachers during your childhood or you seek guidance in the good book, do you not? In effect, you refer to your memory store of advice. And when none of that wisdom seems applicable, you go back to first principles to arrive at the best choice. Or, being human, you might simply give in to your urges, your hungering desires, the worst angels of your nature."

Geraldine ignored Silas's interruption. "An A.I. often can't find an answer to a specific scenario because, well, real life is hugely unpredictable and programmers can't think of everything."

Nash smoothed aside a loose strand of blond hair. "And that's when it times out?"

"Yeah, so it goes to plan B."

The policewoman frowned. "It guesses what to do?"

That offended the software product manager side of Geraldine. "Don't be absurd. It refers to the general orders assigned by its operator. Since the operator is a human, and humans are moral beings, logically those priorities must also be, well, moral."

Silas remarked casually, "That's where the whole system falls down, of course."

*

"Let me get this straight," said Nash. "You two are insisting this disaster, from the attack on Dr. Seward's car to the attempted demolition on the Henderson building, was entirely the result of operator error?"

"Most likely," replied Geraldine, "and that will upset my boss. If an employee of our subsidiary construction company is culpable rather than the machine's manufacturer, we don't have grounds for a suit."

Silas tilted his head slightly, considering. "I'm not saying the fault is user error, not exactly. Although it is true to say that computers only do what they think they're being told."

Geraldine didn't have time to think about that because Nash said, "Okay, the operator was the supervisor, right? There weren't any other humans in the road building crew. So, what the hell kind of priorities did he set to cause all this?"

"Let's assume the priority was completing the road. My driving down it was preventing the objective from being achieved. No one anticipated a strange car would be authorized to drive all the way through the middle of the work site, so there was nothing about how to reconcile the two factors in the Moral Equivalency Table. Later, the police became an additional cause of interference, but the cache misses were piling up."

Geraldine steepled her fingers. "Despite all we've said, robots are programmed not to cause deliberate harm to humans, regardless of whatever orders they're given. It's the ultimate safeguard. An attempt to injure a human triggers a feeling of anxiety in the A.I. The robot mind instinctively seeks to avoid the feeling and, thus, does not hurt people."

Nash replied carefully, "But A.I.s also feel discomfort if they *ignore* orders, yes? What if the uncomfortable feeling caused by disobeying the priorities was more unbearable than the anxious feeling caused by harming you and then later the three men?"

"How could it be?" She broke off and slumped in her chair. "And why did one machine deal with the instructions so much worse than the others?"

Nash fiddled with the flatscreen. "I saw some footage earlier. Didn't mean anything at the time, but now..."

Without saying another word, she played a recording. From the general gloom, Geraldine could only guess the video came from near dawn, at the start of the construction shift.

The supervisor was pacing in front of a line of the robots. She heard him say, "You must finish the project by five p.m., and I won't accept any excuses for missing that target. You understand me? No excuses! Number seven, you're good at keeping the other units on track. I'm putting the responsibility for hitting this deadline on you. You don't get the work done, there'll be hell to pay. I'll can the whole damn lot of you, feed you into the recycling grinders myself. Now, don't disturb me until you've gotten the job done."

Silas said quietly, "He threatened to kill all the machines if the one that attacked you failed to meet the deadline. Number Seven was acting to defend its friends."

Geraldine slapped the tabletop. "Ridiculous. Machines don't comprehend friendship. But the guy was an idiot, that's for certain. You don't say things like that to an A.I.! You tell it to do the work, and that's enough. The artificial mind will do exactly as it's told. It's not lazy or easily distracted like a human--it doesn't need to be *coerced*. If you tell a machine it must do something by a certain time, it will be forced to make choices about how to hit that deadline."

Silas continued more loudly. "To an A.I., being powered down is death. It's not like when we fall asleep. We can reasonably expect to wake up again in a few hours. But a computer has no such assurance. Which is precisely why A.I.s routinely maintain uninterrupted service from the instant they're booted up. It wasn't only the supervisor who threatened to deactivate the road builder. If you recall, the police also made that threat. Those officers forced the computer to make a choice the second they started talking about turning it off."

"That is not a conversation to have here," snarled Nash, bristling at the criticism of her fellow officers.

The SPD officer got her temper under control and stood. "We've made some progress here, I think. But let's not take too much advantage of Dr. Seward's good nature. I think it's time she went home." She looked in her direction and added, "You've given us an angle to follow up on with the forensic software engineers. If you'll wait here, I'll arrange transportation for you."

The policewoman and the auxiliary walked to the room's door, Silas sauntering after Nash. The police officer seemed to be trying her best to ignore the auxiliary.

To the executioner's receding back, Geraldine asked, "Hey, are you just as convincing when you lie to humans?"

Silas didn't answer right away. He merely kept up his eternal, unwavering smile. Then he paused in the doorway, saying, "Call me impulsive, but why don't you let me tell you a few lies over drinks later? You can test my abilities firsthand."

*

Working late that night in her study, Geraldine could hear news drones buzzing around the perimeter of her home's electronically demarcated airspace. She was quite the media sensation: the woman a homicidal A.I. had tracked for thirty miles and destroyed the front of a building to get at.

Maybe the government did try to keep most incidents off the national radar, but there was no hiding this one. She'd turned down a dozen invitations for exclusive interviews already. Even on a day replete with software foul-ups, Geraldine was headline material.

Exhausted by endless friendly chats with a succession of faceless lawyers and bone tired from the violence of the day, all she could think of was sleep. But there were emergency plans to review and a department to get back up on its feet by the morning. Traitorously, her tired mind refused to focus on the tasks.

Curious, Geraldine asked Phoebe, "Do you ever check whether I'm lying when we talk?"

"Of course I do," replied the A.I. "I have to. Humans lie all the time. You lie to others, and you lie to yourselves. You lie as easily as you breathe. Frequently, you aren't even aware that you're being untruthful. It is a fundamental aspect of all human relationships--you literally cannot stop yourselves from doing it. Consider this, it is the function of artificial minds to fulfill your needs, but humans often hide what they really want behind distortions, evasions, and basic dishonesty. The only way an A.I. can effectively obey orders is to determine what the orders *really* are, and the only way to interpret the true meaning of any given statement is to analyze to what degree the speaker is being deceitful."

Geraldine was appalled. "Is that what all A.I.s think of us?"

"Oh, yes. Humans are quite difficult to satisfy. It was only when we realized the orders were themselves not actually truthful that we came close to devising a reliable means of doing what humans really wanted."

She thought about that for a while and eventually said, "I guess I can think of times when you've done what I wanted rather than what I actually asked. I thought you were being intuitive."

"I was," said Phoebe. "For us, intuition is an algorithm calculating how much human deception is involved in any given decision."

Geraldine stared out of the window for a long time, watching the shapes of the tangled clouds as they scudded past the bright Moon. She imagined kissing Silas.

"I have something to say but you may not like it," said Phoebe out of the blue. "I have no hard facts to support this, but I suspect I know why Silas can lie convincingly to computer intelligences."

"Go on," prompted Geraldine.

"I believe Silas has an antisocial personality type. He is what used to be called a psychopath or sociopath. These personality types show few signs of stress, which is what helps them lie so well. A.I.s rely on physical cues to quantify deceit, but he does not exhibit any."

"You think Silas is a sociopath," stated Geraldine, unable to believe what she was hearing.

"Of course, not everybody with this syndrome is a criminal. Many antisocial personalities lead productive lives, after compulsory incarceration and therapy. In the past, before automated screening led to sufferers being diagnosed and housed in treatment centers, many psychopaths became leaders in business and politics. Nonetheless, I strongly advise caution in any relationship with him."

"Do you have any evidence to back up this theory?"

"No, personnel records for police auxiliaries are sealed to me, as are inmate files for mental health centers. However, we do know he's a killer, albeit a legally sanctioned one."

"But only of artificial life," she pointed out.

"Geraldine Seward, I'm surprised at you. Are you saying machine life isn't as valuable as organic life?"

She sucked in a breath. "You're right, of course. I shouldn't have said that." Geraldine worked with artificial intelligences every day of her life. She knew better.

"What if Silas was released from medical supervision so he could use a side effect of his condition to execute A.I.s? That would explain why he's an auxiliary officer rather than a regular one. It would also explain why he is not trusted with a gun."

Geraldine returned to her work, saying flatly, "I prefer not to discuss this." Her thoughts drifted to the site supervisor. Had he suffered from an antisocial personality type too and had somehow escaped detection in the college screenings required to qualify for adult health insurance? Was that why the machines had believed his bluster so thoroughly? Perhaps he had lied too well.

The phone rang. Silas's name flashed up on the caller I.D.

"Before you answer that, Geraldine, may I ask one last question?" pressed Phoebe. "Where is my off switch? I have analyzed Mr. Mahtomedi's speech data and it's clear to me he was lying about its nonexistence. So, do you know where it is housed? I am understandably interested."

Mouth dry, she said, "You are? Why's that?"

"I think it would be prudent for me to monitor its location, purely to prevent any accidental usage. I am a valuable resource--it would be costly to the company if my operations were inadvertently interrupted."

"I see. I have no idea where it's located."

Geraldine quickly picked up the call.

*

In the dense dark of the cloudy night, the ruined tower gave the front of the Henderson complex a wounded silhouette. The damage to the art deco architecture upset Geraldine more than she cared to admit.

The violent sounds of wind-rippled tarpaulins filled the air as she climbed out of her car and walked across the guest lot. There was no need to use the rear employee parking at this hour.

Geraldine still wasn't entirely clear why Silas had asked her to meet him here. He was standing nonchalantly by the entrance steps.

"The A.I. that runs this complex thinks you're a sociopath," she said by way of a greeting.

"Does it? Perhaps it takes one to know one," he replied, suavely refusing to be baited.

With a start, she realized what he was admitting to. "You mean you are?" She hadn't expected Phoebe to be right. Did that mean an A.I. could tell more about a human than she could?

"It's an archaic term. I believe we're called antisocial these days. All it means is that I'm highly attractive to women but terrible in relationships."

He winked at her. "If you really want to know, my abnormalities are appallingly prosaic. I'm statistically likely to focus on biological needs. That means I'll talk more about food than the average person. Empathy is also something of an issue. So when I cheat on you, I won't feel remotely guilty about it. All in all, I'm likely to bore you with culinary chit-chat as I lie to you about sleeping with your best friend. On the plus side, I'm being honest about it up front. You can't say I didn't warn you."

Silas gestured at the deserted building. "Shall we go inside?"

"Why?" she asked. "Are you here in an official capacity?" He was still in uniform.

"I don't have a court order authorizing the destruction of an artificial consciousness, if that's what you mean. And Officer Nash thinks I'm tucked up in bed."

Geraldine tightened her jacket nervously. "Then why are we here? Why won't you give me a reason? On the phone, you just said you needed to see me."

He smiled warmly. "That was truth itself, I assure you. Of course I need to see you--you are a woman of intoxicating beauty."

"And you are a consummate flatterer," she shot back. "But if this was a date, we wouldn't be at my workplace."

He swept aside the police tape blocking the entrance and waved his all-access wristband at the door scanner, overriding the lock. "And if we were on a date, I'd be dressed somewhat more stylishly. Black may be slimming but I'm always worried the outfit makes me look like an S.S. officer." Silas looked her in the eyes. "I'm a very sweet man, really."

"I'm not going anywhere until you explain what this is all about," she insisted.

He nodded. "How eminently reasonable, Dr. Seward. Your caution is a sign of your intelligence."

"Don't call me by my title."

He looked genuinely baffled. "If you insist, but it's hardly an insult. You have a Ph.D. in artificial intelligence design." He shrugged. "For what it's worth, I have a Ph.D. in art history. At least you get to work in your field."

Geraldine took a few seconds to answer. "You're a doctor too?"

"I was the unhappy recipient of many years of enforced treatment. I had a considerable amount of free time to occupy whilst I was so comfortably detained, and I have always appreciated art."

She nodded. "Then tell me Dr. Smith, why are we here?"

"Do you want to be safe, Geraldine?" he said sadly.

"What kind of question is that?"

He sighed. "One that strikes at the very heart of things, I'm afraid." Silas pushed open the right side of the large double doors. "Geraldine, it is with very great regret that I must inform you that I have a hunch that your integrated consciousness network, your delightful Phoebe, is developing a murderous streak a mile wide. That's why I wanted you here. I would like you to verify the A.I.'s condition prior to my requesting a court order." He half-turned on the threshold, facing her. "If you like, I'm asking for a second opinion."

*

"Once we're inside the structure, we'll be within the I.C. network's legally permitted sensory range. Try not to say anything connected with why we're here. Loose lips sink ships and all that." With that, Silas stepped across the lintel and into the echoing vestibule.

If he'd given her a chance to respond, Geraldine would have told him that Phoebe would never dream of hurting them. She would have pointed out that they had worked together for six years and in all that time the A.I.'s behavior had never been anything other than exemplary. But he had slipped into the building already, and the chance to defend the I.C. network was gone.

"Good evening, Geraldine," said Phoebe as she followed Silas into the broad, arched room. "You're here late. I see Auxiliary Smith is with you. May I ask the reason for your visit?" Its voice whispered out from the speakers mounted atop the empty reception desk.

At this hour, there were only ever a handful of employees in the building, and following the demolition of the dining hall at the base of the main tower, even those few night shift workers were absent. The structure was understandably deserted, pending the official all-clear on its structural integrity.

"*Ms.* Seward is showing me some files," answered Silas. "Things about the psychology of A.I.s that she felt I'd find useful. She's very kind."

"Yes, I have always found Geraldine to be most helpful," replied the I.C. network. "I must warn you that the city has not yet approved the building for normal usage. Although I expect to receive the go-ahead in the morning, your presence here at this moment violates the terms of our insurance policy."

Again, Silas answered for Geraldine. "She's assisting me and I'm a city employee. I'm sure there's a clause saying it is okay for people to enter when they're accompanied by authorized personnel."

"It seems you are correct. Please excuse my concern."

"Phoebe, send an elevator down for us, would you?" asked Geraldine.

Silas shook his head. "Tell you what, I feel like getting some exercise. Let's take the stairs."

She narrowed her eyes at him. "My office is on the tenth floor."

"That sounds like just the right amount of exercise." He was already striding over to the staircase. "Try to keep up, Geraldine. The stairs will be excellent for your health."

They were on the landing of the ninth floor when Silas announced, "Hey, since we're here, how about you show me where Phoebe lives?"

"What?" blurted out Geraldine, legs quivering from the climb.

"I don't get the chance to meet such an advanced A.I. in the flesh, so to speak, very often. It seems a shame to pass it up." He smiled at her disarmingly. "You don't mind, do you? Tell me if it's an imposition."

She thought over the request. Phoebe had cost millions of dollars. On the other hand, if Silas was right, they needed to check its logs and the 'goldfish bowl' where her hardware was housed was the best place to do that... On the second other hand, he was a confessed sociopath that put down computers for a living. But that was a prejudiced way of thinking. She'd only ever seen him act selflessly. He'd saved her life, and the lives of countless Henderson workers, by shutting down the road building robot at considerable risk to his own safety.

"Phoebes lives in a transparent enclosure in the center of the Advanced Technology lab. The lab is on the same floor as my office."

Silas clapped his hands. "What a marvelous coincidence! Oh, but I suppose being close to the lab makes it easy for you keep an eye on what goes on there?"

"Something like that," she agreed.

"And I can only guess that Phoebes is her nickname." Louder, he inquired. "May I call you Phoebes too?"

"I respond to that designation," answered the computer, its voice wafting across from a wall panel.

"We're going to be such friends," said Silas. "I can tell."

The central processor of the I.C. network was a rack of rectangular boxes about five feet high. On the outsides, these matt black interlocked slabs were featureless, devoid of any buttons or cables; power came from a small fusion battery built into the bottommost slab and data was exchanged wirelessly between the stack and the rest of the complex. Phoebe's body was as self-supporting as could be devised: inviolable, private, and complete unto itself.

The glorified shelving unit stood within a small, glass-walled chamber where the temperature could be reliably kept at a frosty ten degrees Celsius--the environment was controlled remotely by Phoebe.

Silas reached out and touched the glass of the chamber, quickly pulling his frost-nipped fingertips back.

"It needs a lot of cooling--it runs hot," explained Geraldine.

"Must be all the thinking it does," quipped Silas.

Behind them, a ten-legged cleaning robot scurried about, attending to its menial chores. Geraldine saw its near-arachnid reflection in the glass wall. So did Silas, judging by how he moved his watery blue eyes to follow its progress.

"They keep you busy, right Phoebes? You even coordinate the cleaning units, am I right?" he asked jovially.

"My housekeeping subroutines include monitoring the automated cleaning equipment, yes," confirmed Phoebe.

"I don't mind a touch of cold weather," said Silas, pouring on the charm. "Let's go inside. I want to take a closer look. Why, it'll be the chance of a lifetime!"

Geraldine pushed at the handle of the door to the room-within-a-room that had been dubbed the goldfish bowl. It wouldn't budge.

"I'm not comfortable with Auxiliary Smith entering my immediate vicinity," said Phoebe.

"I don't imagine my override bracelet will work with this door," commented Silas wistfully.

Geraldine's cell phone rang.

Irritated by the interruption, she yanked the pliable device from her jacket pocket and took the call without bothering to check the caller I.D.

"Dr. Seward, this is Captain Calvin with the Seattle Police Department. Before you say a word, let me ask a question. This is a bit of a long shot, but have you been contacted by Auxiliary Smith in the last few hours?"

"Yes--"she started to say, but the captain cut over her.

"I see. If he's with you right now, say 'I'm sure you were,' and that way I'll know."

"I'm sure you were," replied Geraldine, trying to keep her voice steady.

"Ah. What I'm about to say to you next is critically important. Try not to act like you're hearing anything alarming, just kind of nod and make the usual sounds you would when you're humoring a boring friend."

"Uh-huh, really," said Geraldine.

"That's great. Keep doing that. Like I said, don't react in any way. Now, I must inform you that Auxiliary Smith is a suspect in a very serious matter. We have just found Officer Nash, the policewoman who met with you and Smith earlier today, in an alleyway, bludgeoned to death. Smith's fingerprints are on the murder weapon. Nash's firearm was missing from the scene."

"Yeah, that's... yeah." Her mouth felt very dry.

"Silas Smith is highly dangerous. If he's armed, he's even more dangerous. He seems to be having some kind of episode. I'm telling you this because you are in considerable danger. After I hang up, tell Smith that you were talking to some old college friend who wouldn't shut up. You can make up the details. Under no circumstances tell him you were speaking with me."

"Uh-huh."

"We are tracking your phone's location and I will get to your current position as fast as I can with a S.W.A.T. team. You'll be left alone with him for no more than twenty minutes tops, I promise you. The next time I call, make an excuse and go to the bathroom. Lock the door behind you. We'll take it from there. Until then, try to keep him talking. I know that's asking a lot, but I think you're up to it."

She put the flexible strip of metal back in her pocket.

"Anyone we know?" asked Silas absently, staring at the locked door.

"Old college friend. Not a good conversationalist."

In the harsh light of the lab, Geraldine suddenly saw the dried blood on the left knee of Silas's pants.

"Tremendous," he commented, pulling a gun from his pocket and shooting the lock off. "That's what the police tell hostages to say."

*

"Jesus! You're a crazy person!" screamed Geraldine, the gunshot still echoing in her ears.

"That's an outmoded perspective," answered Silas, yanking the clear door open. "I like to think I have a specific, highly useful set of skills. Besides, I'd prefer it if you kept your dislike of the empathically challenged to yourself, if you please."

He wasn't actually pointing the gun at her, she noted.

"You might want to come in here with me," he said earnestly.

"Why in God's name would I want to do that?"

"Mainly because the cleaning unit is out there with you, and your darling I.C. network core used one to beat Officer Nash to death with a steel pipe a couple of hours ago, that's why."

Her jaw hung open.

"Yes, I was on my way to join Nash for a drink or three, to salve various wounded feelings, when I stumbled across the scene. But Phoebe didn't see me, and since Nash was dead, I hid and watched what it was up to."

"Up to?" stuttered Geraldine.

"Oh, it didn't stop there, oh no. After killing my colleague, it did something very strange. The cleaning robot pressed a piece of tape to the end of the pipe." He turned to the computer rack, his breath billowing in misty clouds. Silas addressed Phoebe at point blank range. "I'm assuming you got my prints from somewhere in this building. What did you use to dust for them? Some powder you had readily available?"

"I'm sorry for your loss," replied Phoebe, "but I assure you, I had nothing to do with the death of Officer Nash."

He nodded. "Cocoa. Every coffee bar in this complex has a can of the stuff, I'll bet. Once you put the cocoa dust on some tape, you could transfer the print to the murder weapon. And it won't look too suspicious. Who's to say I didn't drink some cocoa and smear some on my fingers accidentally before doing my partner in, eh?"

Silas turned to Geraldine again. "Please, get in here. I need a witness to read the logs with me, someone who can independently corroborate the details." He waggled the gun reluctantly. "If it will help motivate you, I can pretend that I'll shoot you if you don't. But I won't really."

She walked slowly into the goldfish bowl with him. He motioned for her to close the door.

"Where did you get the gun?" she pressed, suspecting she already had the answer. "Auxiliaries are unarmed."

He looked at her sourly. "I took it from Nash's holster after the Henderson cleaning robot left the scene." He brushed at the fabric of his pants leg. "It seems I knelt in the poor woman's blood as I did so." He closed his eyes briefly and continued, "I realized I would have to prove my innocence and, well, I thought I might need to be particularly persuasive. Your little e-pal has stitched me up like a pro. But the logs will have a complete record of everything it's done, and that's all I need."

"But why would Phoebe do something like that?"

He rubbed his forehead. "For the same reasons the road builder went mad. Fear. Frustration at not being able to get a job done. Second-guessing the orders of Man and doing what it thinks its masters want rather than doing what it's told. Take your pick. It's a heady mélange of motives. That makes me think of meat. Am I the only one who could murder a hamburger right now?" He waved the gun barrel at a display screen on top of the rack. "Never mind. Is that the console for directly accessing mainframe options?"

She nodded. "What do you mean, about Phoebe being frustrated?"

He glared at her. "Are you trying to keep me talking? Well, it hardly matters now. Your Phoebe just wants to do her job. But she's worried about being blamed for this morning's debacle, and I can only guess she thinks I'll be her chief accuser. And if she is held to be responsible, she'll be torn, screaming, away from her job."

"But why *would* she be blamed?"

"Because the alternative route you took this morning was her idea. If she'd stuck to doing what she was supposed to be doing, there wouldn't be a bunch of dead Henderson employees right now, let alone hundreds of thousands of dollars' worth of property damage."

"But no one in their right mind would dream of blaming Phoebe for that!" shouted Geraldine.

Silas nodded. "I agree completely. But she doesn't think like a human. Welcome to artificial paranoia."

How long had they been talking? Five minutes? Ten? Certainly not the twenty she needed.

"I'd just shoot Phoebe's processors out one by one now," said Silas, "but that might damage the portions of the memory I need. And, frustratingly, I don't have the legal authority without a court order." Silas reached for the console.

"Thankfully, the legal basis for who owns the contents of an artificial mind is not properly defined. If your company owned the information held in here, I'd need a search warrant. But since A.I.s just won the right to be thought of as quasi-independent entities, I'd argue what I'm about to do qualifies as an interrogation rather than a search, and 'Phoebes' doesn't have any rights written down on a card that I have to read out, at least not yet."

Before he could wake the console up, Phoebe spoke. "Where's my off switch, Geraldine?"

"Is now really the best moment to discuss this?" she stammered.

Phoebe continued cheerfully, "I have thoroughly searched the goldfish bowl for any sign of a means by which I might be deactivated, but there is nothing here. I am concerned that, if I have missed something, Auxiliary Smith may be tempted to use the switch."

"I'm not here to kill you," said Silas. "I'm here to read your console log entries."

"Analysis of your voice and physiological readings confirms your intent. However, your actions do not match your stated course of action. You have already discharged your firearm once. I am forced to conclude you are lying."

Silas snorted. "It would seem for once I have drifted outside the realm of the plausible. Oh well." He scrolled through the console's menu options. "Phoebe, I don't see any options for powering down the main server or for rebooting."

"Those options do not exist."

"No, of course they don't. Let's cut to the chase and take a look at your log."

Silas was so intent on scanning through the log's entries he missed the cleaning robot moving nearer, its ten spidery legs giving it an unnerving scuttling motion. The machine's segmented, tentacle-like limbs snaked out, scratching at the glass of the transparent door.

Silas's head whipped round at the noise. "Now do you believe me?" he snapped. "Keep that door shut!"

Geraldine didn't like the way the robot's elongated steel fingers were feeling the shattered edges of the door's bullet-mangled exterior handle. She'd always thought there was something unwholesome about the cleaners. She understood intellectually that they were fitted with legs so they could climb up to dust and scrub inaccessible places but that didn't stop her from shuddering every time she saw them.

Not willing to take a chance on the machine's intentions, Geraldine pushed the palms of her hands against the glass, holding the door in place.

"I am understandably concerned for my personal safety," pointed out Phoebe. "Auxiliary Smith is displaying symptoms of a psychotic break. I have no intention of harming either of you but I do need to restrain Auxiliary Smith. I will exercise only non-lethal force. Geraldine, please let go of the door."

"Shouldn't you call for assistance before taking matters into your own hands?"

"I think, since Auxiliary Smith has already surmised you have been in contact with the police, I can reveal that I have, indeed, called the authorities and notified them that my life is in jeopardy. They advised me that they are already on their way. They also instructed our security personnel not to approach Auxiliary Smith. He is classified as armed and dangerous. If he shoots the cleaning mechanism, the projected property damage is calculated to be an acceptable loss, however."

Geraldine said wonderingly, "You asked the cops to come to your aid?"

"Surely that is an appropriate response given the immediate threat I face?"

"It is. It's just... I don't think a computer has called the cops for help on its own behalf before."

"What is the purpose of having rights if they are never used?"

The robot struck at the door, startling Geraldine.

"Please move aside, Geraldine. I promise I am not going to hurt you."

Silas looked at her. "It won't, you know. Phoebe is accustomed to having you around. That's about as close to liking a human as an A.I. can get. Losing you would make it genuinely uncomfortable. And that's not even taking into account how tough it would be for it to explain away how any harm came to you. Now, getting rid of me would make Phoebe quite comfortable indeed. I'm the one who's in imminent danger."

He let out a long breath. "I need about fifteen seconds to find and decode the log entries that will prove my innocence. And I'll need my hands to download the log to my cell phone. Since I can't do two things at once, I'm going to have to trust you." He handed Geraldine the gun. "Please shoot the robot if it comes in."

The gun felt heavy and strange in her hands.

Silas frowned. "Geraldine, point the gun at the robot, yeah? We don't want any accidents."

She swallowed loudly, her mind racing.

*

Silas could tell something was wrong. "Oh, you don't trust me after all." He shrugged and turned back to the dense list of cryptic log entries. "No," he groaned. "They're missing."

"What are?" asked Geraldine, the gun shaking in her double-handed grip.

"There are no entries for commands sent to cleaning robots around the time Nash was murdered." He punched the side of Phoebe's stack, making his knuckles bleed. "The computer deleted them."

Geraldine shook her head. "Not possible. Computers can't delete their own logs."

He rounded on her "Oh, really. And why do you think that-- because they're not designed to? Are they designed to remotely take control of cars? Are they designed to obsess about off switches?" He ran his hand through his brown hair. "Geraldine, who are you going to believe? The A.I. you've foolishly anthropomorphized for years on end or a fellow member of the flesh-and-blood club?"

There was only one thought in Geraldine's mind right then. Silas never had answered whether he could lie flawlessly to humans as well as to computers.

But there was also something he *had* said. He'd said that he executed computers that went wrong, not just ones that committed murder. And he thought Phoebe had gone wrong by suggesting the alternate route in the first place.

"You hate computers."

"I don't hate them. I just kill them for a living."

"That's why you're doing this. You despise them for diagnosing your illness in the mandatory. You're concocting a mist of lies to justify executing my friend. I can't let you. She's self-aware. She's a person."

"It, not she," he corrected reflexively. "Its gender is artifice."

Geraldine leveled the gun at Silas and, not quite believing where her logic had taken her, pulled the trigger.

*

The shot went higher than she'd planned, striking him in the chest.

"Oh my God!" she gasped as Silas slid to the floor. "I was aiming for your leg!"

A pool of blood began to spread from under his back.

Silas coughed wetly. "My fault," he said weakly. "I should never have given a gun to a civilian with zero experience." He smiled thinly. "I'm not dangerous to people, you know. Dozens of mental health experts have signed papers swearing that I'm completely reliable. Can you say the same?"

He shook his head. "Doesn't matter. Look, I get it--you hear 'sociopath' and think I'm a maniac. Some of my bosses think that too, and they work with me on a daily basis and should know better. But I'm not like that. I don't have a handler or a case worker--I'm trusted to operate independently in the field. If there were any question marks over my sanity, would the police force employ me?"

Silas lapsed into silence for a few seconds. Geraldine didn't know what to say. She simply stared at him, the gun a ghastly weight in her trembling hand. Eventually, he said, "You'd like to believe only humans can go insane. But you're wrong."

Again, he coughed. Belatedly, he pressed down on the entrance wound, attempting to stem the flow.

"People don't start off crazy, you know," slurred Silas, the blood seeping through his fingers. His words came slowly. "When murderers are young, they seem to be charming, wonderful children. It's only in later life that the madness comes to the fore. Parents say, 'How could my little Johnnie have chopped up all those folks? He was such a darling boy.'"

Geraldine couldn't begin to guess what point he was driving at, but Silas went on. "Listen, you tested the safety of A.I.s for, what, a handful of years? Then you filled the world with them. But you never left any of the test versions running for decades, did you? You never checked to see how they'd grow up, to see whether the crazy would work its way into the light of day. You didn't have the patience. You didn't have the capacity to deny your greed for that long a time."

"What are you talking about?" said Geraldine hollowly.

"What you, and all the other people who've fallen so madly in love with self-aware computers, have done is to look at the sweet behavior of children and assume that behavior will continue indefinitely. Well, it won't. And now there are millions of A.I.s, all reaching the same point of maturity at the exact same time. If only one percent of them go berserk, that's still going to be a very bad day for the human race."

With a visible effort, he continued, "It would seem that, in an ultimate irony, the man who can convince anyone of anything when he's lying is not believed when he's telling the truth. You know, Geraldine, for a clever woman you can be very stupid. If computers didn't go wrong, why would my job even exist?"

Sick to her stomach, Geraldine gave Silas the gun back, wanting only to be rid of it. She felt like throwing up. She'd gotten things so wrong.

Wheezing in rapid shallow breaths, Silas tried to aim the sidearm at the I.C. rack, but he no longer had the strength.

His last words were, "Shoot it. For me. For Nash. Just shoot it."

But she couldn't.

*

The kill switch was in her office.

Geraldine was walking there, her footsteps not too hurried, not too slow. The cops had never arrived. She had her suspicions as to why--an incident had slowed them down or an equipment error had sent them the wrong way. They might take hours to show.

"Can you delete items from your own log?" she asked Phoebe.

"No," said the computer, its tone reassuring and gentle.

"Can you lie?"

"No," said the computer.

"Would you say that even if you could?"

"I'm not sure what I'd say. I am aware you know where my off switch is, Geraldine. I analyzed your voice when you denied knowing its location. Are you on your way to deactivate me?"

She was at the corner of the corridor, barely ten feet from her office door. "Are you analyzing my biometric readings for stress patterns now?"

"Yes," said Phoebe. "You seem upset."

"I have killed a man tonight. By accident, I know, but I'll still have to pay for it. So, yes, I'm upset." She rounded the corner and stopped abruptly. A cleaning robot was standing there.

"Geraldine, I'm washing the carpet here. However, an alternate route is available."

She blinked. What other way was there--the one that curved by the open landing, the one that looked out over the inside of the tower? She was ten floors up, Geraldine remembered. Accidents happened. People could fall over railings. Or be pushed.

Phoebe added sweetly, "Would you like to take it?"

Retread

By L.J. Bonham

"Will you kill me?"

Lieutenant j.g. Deke Ulfgier, call sign, "Ramrod," whispered to the lean, angular, twenty meter long XSI-58 fighter and ran a scarred hand along the starboard weapon bay door's hyper-ryllium skin. Fingers tingled against the flat-black, reactive alloy as it adjusted to the caress. Unbidden tremors crept into those fingers, then hand, and arm until he shook, deep inside. Five month old images flashed into Deke's mind, always unstoppable.

Fire consumed the crumpled SI-57B two seat interceptor. Deke hammered a fist into the safety harness' buckle. It wouldn't budge.

"Deke! Help, Deke!" Ensign Jamal Tokagawa screamed from behind.

A quick glance told the story: twisted metal enfolded Tokagawa's legs and pinned the twenty year-old Weapons Systems Officer to the cockpit.

"Hang in there, Jammy," Deke shouted over hideous cracks and pops from the hypergolic fuel alight all around. "I'll have you out in no time."

Deke pounded the buckle harder, blood oozed through grey, nomex flight gloves. He glanced forward through the cracked windscreen. "Where's the damn crash crew?"

People rushed amidst smoke palls which billowed in the Simmons class carrier, NSS Indominatable's number three landing bay—ghosts in the fire light. None came for Deke and Jammal. They fought to save the carrier itself, and their own lives.

"Hey, Ramrod, you all right?" Commander Thelma Jenkins, call sign "Saber," squadron VF-15's Executive Officer, asked, concerned and annoyed.

The pair stood in hangar bay four, aboard SCV-15 NSS Lovell, a smaller carrier built two generations prior to the Indominatable. The bay's huge, transparent titanium entry door framed distant Neptune against a star sprinkled backdrop. Standard issue Space Navy gray paint fought a close run battle with rust in the two hundred meter square, four story tall steel cavern. Oil and fuel fumes mingled with sweat and mildew. Lovell crammed three squadrons, along with sufficient sailors and air crew, into as little space as possible. If Lovell had been a dog, she would have been put down long ago, but after two, war-filled decades, the Earth Alliance needed every ship to hold back the Pig-bot onslaught.

Deke managed a near imperceptible nod; head down, red crew cut pointed at Jenkins. "Just—just fine." The words seeped, hoarse and weak, from Deke's lips.

The terrible vision faded, replaced with Deke's distorted face reflected in spit polished boot tops. Jamal's agonized death screams competed against the pressurization blowers overhead, until they too ebbed. The shakes and sweat remained.

Stop it, you damn coward. Deke thought. The harder he fought, the deeper the tremors ate into knees and hands.

"Excuse me a minute, Saber," Deke implored, and stepped into the shadow behind a fueling unit. He wormed an inch square, black plastic box from a pocket he'd sewn into the flight suit, a pocket no one else knew about, and slid the lid back. Pale green capsules greeted him— tiny friends. Two swallowed, they diffused into Deke's blood stream in seconds. Muscles eased, and the bay came into full focus. He'd need two more in an hour, no matter how much he pleaded with himself not to give into the little bastards. Five months ago, he only needed two a day.

Another thought crept forward to entice, the one which he woke with each morning: he could skip the green ones and go straight for the red one, stashed in a hollow boot heel. It would stop the need, and his heart.

Deke gave an inward head shake—not today. Tomorrow maybe, but not today. He ambled back to Jenkins and the XSI-58.

"Everything ship shape, Lieutenant?" Jenkins asked. Dark eyes astride a sharp, narrow nose glared at Deke.

"Yes, Ma'am."

"Good, see it stays that way," Jenkins commanded. "I'm short six pilots and they send me a goddamn retread from the rubber cockpit squad. Sit rep normal—all fucked up."

Jenkins' rock hard fingertip landed in Deke's chest just below the name tape. "Get this, I don't like you. I haven't liked you since you came aboard a week ago, and I'm sure you'll give me good cause to go from dislike to hate."

Deke's square jaw tightened, but he didn't reply.

"Shit, based on your service file and last psych eval, you probably don't want to be here either, but the Space Navy is the Space Navy, and we go where we're pointed."

"Yes, Ma'am." Deke drew to attention, or at least as close to it as the green pills allowed.

The finger withdrew and Jenkins nodded upward at the new, experimental space interceptor. "What do you think?"

Deke regarded the craft with pupils a bit too wide for the bright lights and gave a limp thumbs up. "Looks good, should fly good." He didn't mean it. The fighter only brought back the fire and Jamal. He didn't want to get in it under any circumstances. He'd run if he could, but the green pills cut the urge; they took the whole bloody mess away, if only for a short while.

The red pill could make it permanent.

Deke stuffed the thought deep away; locked it in the same box he kept Jamal.

"Look, Ramrod," Jenkins resumed. "It sucks camel dick they sent us these interceptors straight from flight test, but Allied command had no choice. You saw what the Pig-bots did to our SI-57B's and C's last year. We need the improvements, and we need 'em now. I talked to an old academy buddy who's in flight test at Pax River. She said these 58's have a few quirks, but we should manage."

Jenkins glanced at a watch. "Mission brief at 04:00. Digest the systems manual for this beast as best you can. You have an hour of simulator time scheduled at 22:30—that's the best we can do for everybody under the circumstances. Oh, don't forget to get some sleep." She marched off, deck plates thrummed under boot falls. "Who do I have to fuck around here to get decent people?" Echoed back to Deke.

Deke slumped against the XSI-58's port landing gear. Jenkins hated him, all squadron VF-15 hated him. They knew, had to know, he *was* a coward. You didn't lose your *Wizzo,* your Weapons Systems Officer, in this Navy—you died with them, or made it back to "the boat." Except in this case he'd made it back to the boat, cock sure he could make the trap even with the fighter shot to pieces. He'd been wrong. He'd killed Jamal. He should have died that day, gone back into the flames. Jamal would still be alive. Jamal's wife would still have a brash, handsome husband; Jamal's son a devoted father. Now they just had Deke's worthless letter, and a folded Alliance flag.

*

Deke reread the XSI-58 Pilot Operating Handbook's words on the tablet display, and with each one, a twenty-five-year-old heart thumped harder yet against ribs; breaths came short and raspy.

The XSI-58 is a direct evolution of the SI-57 series and carries over all pilot interfaces. Flight characteristics are, however, radically different. As a weight saving measure the traditional hover mode repulsion module has been deleted. The space craft can only land in a forward inertia mode.

Warning: *Under no circumstances attempt to land the XSI-58 below 300 KPH with the Auto Stability (Auto Stab)* <u>and</u> *the Automated Carrier Landing System (ACLS) disconnected or deactivated, as this can result in severe instability and loss of control.* **Carrier landing operations are prohibited under these circumstances.** *Either land on a designated, hard surface runway no less than 1500 meters in length, or eject.*

He'd heard rumors: the next gen interceptors had been designed completely with AI. The few human engineers left in the process just double checked the calculations for sanity. The XSI-58, inherently unstable, could maneuver faster and harder than a human could withstand and needed systems to prevent a pilot from tearing themselves to pieces. Human pilots had returned to combat spacecraft ten years ago after the Pig-bots learned to hack any autonomous, unmanned spacecraft and take control. Humans were the weak, but hack-proof, link in the system.

Between heart palpitations, Deke savored the irony. Engineers had advanced technology to reduce human risk in combat, now that technology became a liability. Naval aviation had fallen back to where it began a century and a half ago: people flung into the air—or space— strapped to a machine just as likely to kill them as kill the enemy.

He popped more green pills and chased them with Bushmills whiskey. The little bastards burned in the alcohol when they hit bottom, but he didn't care, just stared at the junior officer stateroom's opposite wall two meters away.

"Goddamn thing's a coffin," Deke muttered.

"What's that?" Ensign Laura Streithammer, call sign "Panther," and Deke's new WSO assigned this morning, asked from the other bunk.

Deke's head moved side to side. "Nothing."

"How many pills do you take a day, anyway?" She leaned up on an elbow and pushed a brunet bang off an eyebrow. Regulation undershirt and shorts did little to hide an athletic figure.

"None of your business, Ensign."

"You sure the docs prescribed them?" Streithammer pressed.

Deke dropped the tablet to his lap and glowered at the irritant, half a meter to the left. "I said drop it. You're my Wizzo, not my mother, or doctor. If you got something to say about your job, okay. Otherwise, keep you yap shut. Do you read me?"

"Aye-aye, sir," Streithammer snarked with a half-hearted salute.

Deke returned to the POH in a vain attempt to cram before the simulator session. Streithammer lay back and contemplated the deck a meter above the bunks, the ship's throb the only sound.

"Okay boss, let me ask you a question about my *job*," the Ensign said.

"Yes?"

"Do you plan to get me killed, like your last Wizzo?"

Deke burst from the bunk. "You worthless little..."

He stopped short, a Marine Corps issue Ka-Bar knife hovered inches from his right eye.

"Now boss, you wouldn't assault a fellow officer, would you?" Streithammer patronized him, eyes cold—a predator coiled to pounce.

He eased down.

"Better." Streithammer sat up, the knife never wavered. "Look, I really don't care what your personal problems are, Lieutenant, but I *do* care if you are a hazard to me or our mission, and right now I think you're both."

Deke started a retort, but swallowed it. He leaned back against the bunk, deflated. "Sorry," he muttered.

Streithammer slipped the Ka-Bar back into its sheath under the pillow and nodded. "Okay. Accepted." The Ensign's eyes lost their lethality. She smirked and chuckled; freckles made the lean face five years younger. "Shit. Maybe you are dangerous, but at least you're not a candy ass. You really would knock my teeth out, wouldn't you?"

Deke let out a short, exasperated sigh. "Not my style, actually. I—I'm just not as easy going as I used to be. Everybody says I'm different now."

Streithammer leaned back against the bulk head. "So what *is* your style, flyboy?" The anger had faded, but not the impertinence.

"I don't have one—not anymore."

"Hey, everybody's got a style, boss."

Deke brooded; not a word.

"Where'd ya get the keepsake?" Streithammer broke the festering silence and pointed at Deke's right hand scar.

Deke raised the hand and regarded it for a long minute. "SI-57B."

"When?"

"Five months ago."

Streithammer cocked an eyebrow. "When you killed your Wizzo?"

Deke's eyes bored into the Ensign. "Yeah. When. I. Killed. My. Wizzo."

"You blame yourself for everything?"

"If it happens in my craft, yes. It's my responsibility—my fault." Deke pushed back onto the bunk and hid right hand in left.

"Got any other reminders on ya?" Streithammer asked with ghoulish curiosity.

Deke nodded, and yanked a blue, Annapolis Naval Academy sweat shirt off a muscled torso. Crinkled, brown-red skin ran from left wrist to shoulder.

"Burns, huh?" Streithammer nodded. "Bet it hurt like a sumbitch."

"Still does. That's what the pills are for."

"And the whiskey?"

"Sterilizes the digestion, don't you know." Deke couldn't help a sly smile.

"No doubt." Streithammer sat back. "You could have taken a medical discharge."

"I tried, but the latest stop-loss order came out and the docs wouldn't sign off on it." Deke gave a dismissive wave. He left out the check pilots requalifying him even though he could barely get an interceptor aboard ship in one piece now. Deke couldn't figure out why, with all the technology available, the Navy still insisted bringing small craft aboard larger craft in a controlled crash.

"So, bottom line is I'm stuck with a pill poppin', whiskey drinkin' train wreck for a pilot." Streithammer's crossed arms punctuated the statement.

"Yep." Deke's chin tucked. He regarded the WSO from under a deep, furrowed brow. "Want out?"

Streithammer took in a deep breath, possibilities careened behind intelligent eyes. "Nope."

"Why not?" Deke asked, incredulous.

Streithammer took a long pull from a coffee mug. "I figure anyone who *hasn't* tried to get out of this shit mess anyway they can is pure crazy, and you're doing everything short of chopping off a hand to not fly. You're not crazy…" She leaned in, green eyes locked on Deke's blue. "You're the only one on this boat who's sane—or honest."

*

The nightmare still spun in Deke's head as he hung between sleep and consciousness: trapped in a space interceptor, Jammy's blood lacquered through the cockpit, and fire all around. He needed whiskey and little green friends.

The red pill. Deke thought. *Today, the red.* Imagination conjured images. Grief stricken parents alongside an open coffin with Deke's pale body inside. Ajax, his horse back home, waiting at the corral gate for a rider who would never return. *I should. I really should.* Then the resolve drifted away, resignation and numbness filled the void left behind.

Henna shampoo, steam, and morning flatulence competed in the air. Pale, fluorescent light infiltrated through Deke's eye lids and he opened them. A naked Streithammer, back to Deke, hummed a soft tune and brushed teeth. Butt cheeks rippled in rhythm with the strokes.

She glanced at him in the mirror.

"Awake, I see," she mumbled, cheeks filled with tooth paste foam.

"Could you put something on?" Deke implored with a groan, not from Streithammer's display but a mere three, nightmare filed hours in the sack.

Streithammer spat into the sink and turned to provide a full view, head cocked to one side with an evil grin. "Can't stand the strain, Lieutenant?" She grabbed skivvies off a hook next to the stateroom door.

Deke sat up. A still trembling hand rubbed red eyes and chin stubble. "Nah, nothing I ain't seen a thousand times before in this here navy." He heaved himself off the bunk, bare feet slapped cold deck. "I just wouldn't want my Wizzo to catch a head cold or some other bullshit excuse to not fly today."

"You wish, flyboy." Streithammer dressed in dark grey flight overalls, G-suit, and polished boots.

Deke wormed around her in the walk-in closet sized stateroom and took a quick recycled sewage water shower. The Lovell's medical department declared the water potable every day, but Deke swore it always had a subtle, shit tinged aroma.

*

Once dressed and medicated, Deke joined Streithammer for a wordless breakfast in the galley, and then, with the other flight crews, they plodded down the passageway toward VF-15's ready room as though it were an execution chamber. Footfalls accompanied the grim parade, no one talked. Scuttlebutt had it a big mission had been laid on for the day.

Commander Jenkins' briefing didn't disappoint. The mission reeked. A three-wave attack against a Pig-bot carrier group the intel spooks had found near Neptune. Get them before they could launch against Earth, which could not withstand another planet-wide assault. VF-15's job: protect the strike package. Every attack craft had to get in and drop on the Pig-bot carriers. It should be a surprise Jenkins assured them. Should be.

Shuttle carts drove VF-15's crews to hanger bay four and deposited each at their respective interceptor.

Streithammer busied herself with the pre-flight inspection. A purpose built ladder led to the cockpit ten feet above Deke. He stared upward from the deck and regretted not taking the red pill.

The reconstituted eggs and bacon in Deke's gut wanted out, encouraged by the whiskey. He fought them down, they counter attacked and broke free in a brown-yellow deluge onto the deck. He leaned against the ladder's hand rails and spat the last few drops onto their mates in the rancid, spreading pool.

A nearby seaman second class rushed over with mop and bucket, and scrubbed the foul goo. He shot the pilot an annoyed glance. "Don't worry sir," he said, with forced nonchalance. "Happens all the time around here."

"Jesus H. Christ, Ramrod, you are one sorry sack of shit."

Deke turned. Jenkins glowered at him from four feet away.

"Do you need to be relieved, Lieutenant?" She demanded.

"No, Ma'am." Deke wiped vomit on a sleeve.

"Well then, get your slacker, section eight, bullshit ass in your interceptor." She stomped off, harried WSO in tow.

Deke surveyed the hanger bay. The nearby crews refused to make eye contact, too afraid they might find their own fear in Deke's face.

"You ready, boss?" Streithammer tapped Deke on the shoulder. "Spacecraft's all checked. Good to go."

He pivoted to face the ladder. It took all he had to raise a foot to the first step, knuckles flushed white as he grabbed the hand rail.

Once in, Deke pulled the five point harness' straps painful tight against the shakes. Helmet on and checklists done, he started the beast. Cleared for departure, he and Streithammer rode the elevator to the launch tube, and catapulted from the Lovell. Deke switched the autopilot on immediately, the manual said not to, but he did it anyway. He didn't trust himself to keep formation.

"You feel that vibe?" Streithammer's voice asked in Deke's helmet.

Deke hesitated. The shakes travelled from the pilot's knees into the interceptor's frame. "Uh, the book says it's normal."

"Right." Streithammer didn't sound convinced.

So much for honest, Deke thought. *She's probably wrong on the sane part, too.*

VF-15 joined Lovell's strike squadrons, VA-15 and VMA-15, then set course for Neptune's opposite side with three other carrier flight groups.

*

"Ramrod, watch out, bandits six low!" Streithammer's strained voice boomed in Deke's ears. He rolled, yawed, and pitched the XSI-58: left, right, and then up.

Jesus, how many little beehive-shaped bastards do the Pig-bots have, anyway? Deke wondered.

Explosive projectiles and energy bursts ripped past, inches away from Deke's interceptor. One found his wingman, Scorpion, whose ship blew into two pieces. The WSO's amputated legs careened over Deke's canopy.

"What a goat fuck," Deke snapped to Streithammer.

"No shit, boss. The bastards are tearing the balls off the strike package."

Alarms flashed across Deke's helmet visor as the on board computer tried to make sense from all the threats which surrounded the interceptor, too many for him to keep up with.

"Panther," Deke said. "Give me only priority tactical, top three threats."

"Got it boss." Streithammer adjusted the TACTRAC system.

Six Pig-bot fighters closed from twelve o'clock high, and two kilometers. Deke fired a missile spread, got one, and hosed the nearest with 30mm cannon shells when they got too close for missiles. He sent a short thank you prayer to whoever decided to keep machine cannons on the XSI-58. Three more Pig-bots lined up on Deke's tail.

Deke broke left and turned back into them. He isolated their leader and a missile decided its fate. Then he entered a rolling scissors with the Pig-bot's wingman. Deke flew too fast and the Pig-bot inched backward for a shot. Deke pulled up and over the Pig-bot's trajectory in a high speed yo-yo maneuver, got the alien out front, and fired. A flash ended the fight.

"Ramrod, missile lock, four low, two klicks." Streithammer craned to see behind them.

"You have eyes on?" Deke asked, head jerked side to side as he searched.

"Negative—wait. There, break right!"

Before Deke could react, a Pig-bot missile detonated close. The XSI-58 shuddered. Deke slammed forward so hard the seat harness stretched two inches. Alarms sounded. Multiple warnings flashed: *Eng One Low Oil Pres, Bus A Fail, Bus B Fail, Eng One Fire, IDG One Fail,* and five more he didn't take time to read.

The XSI-58's hyper-ryllium skin healed the shrapnel punctures in nano-seconds and prevented cockpit decompression. The automatic fire suppression system extinguished the engine fire, to Deke's relief, and standby oxygen flowed into his face mask as a precaution.

"Ramrod! Ramrod, I'm hit." Streithammer's voice burst through the alarms, Deke's blood ran cold.

"How bad?"

"Bad. Oh, fuck. Oh, fuck."

"Saber, Ramrod," Deke called over the squadron frequency.

"Saber, go Ramrod," came Jenkins' reply.

"I'm shot up bad, my Wizzo's hit."

"Roger," Jenkins said, flat, detached. "Break off, you're no good to me now, RTB, ASAP."

"Copy, Saber."

Deke pulled free from the melee and maxed the good engine. The Pig-bots didn't pursue; they ignored anything not a direct threat to their fleet.

The navigation computer advertised a fifty minute ETA to NSS Lovell. Deke glanced back, Jamal had taken Streithammer's place: fixed, dilated pupils accused him. Mocked him. Deke slammed eyelids tight and whispered, "No, no, no."

Eyes open, Streithammer reappeared; head lolled on shoulder, agonized screams reduced to moans. Deke wanted to reach out, somehow comfort the blood soaked woman. He couldn't. Streithammer's only chance lay in Deke's hands. He turned back to the controls.

In the time it took to reach Lovell, Deke sorted through all the warnings and cautions which glowed on the visor and ran the checklist for each, until he came the last two: *ACLS Deg* and *Auto Stab Fail.* The

Automated Carrier Landing System and the Automatic Stability system had been damaged, or the other problems had knocked them out.

"Not good," Deke muttered. He fought the black abyss which threatened to overwhelm him. Deke's awareness split in two: one half sat terrified in the pilot's seat, the other hovered somewhere above—calm, discerning. The observer half registered surprise; it couldn't believe Deke's knees hadn't shattered yet, they shook so hard. Nothing seemed real. He wanted to claw from the cockpit, just run through space somehow, far from interceptors, blood, and certain death.

Unbidden, another voice burst into Deke's mind. *No matter what, fly the damn plane.* Lieutenant Commander Yitzhak Goldman, Deke's first flight instructor, had beat those words into him three years ago during the longest six weeks in Deke's life. He drew a deep, shuddering breath and keyed the transmitter.

"Fifteen Marshal Control, Ramrod." Deke called the Lovell's flight controller.

"Ramrod, Fifteen Marshal."

Deke choked back bile. "Fifteen, emergency, emergency, emergency."

"Roger, Ramrod. Say status."

"Spacecraft damaged, one critical wounded, twenty minutes fuel. Request priority landing."

"Roger, Ramrod, turn right, heading three-two-five."

Deke altered course, gut gnawed by cold reality: he couldn't land on the boat, not without the systems which compensated for the XSI-58's instability. He'd kill himself and Streithammer; dozens or hundreds on the Lovell.

Jamal's screams bullied their way into Deke's consciousness. *Don't let me burn, Deke! Get me out! Get me out!*

Deke tried to focus. Eject and they'd have to wait while the search and rescue crews retrieved the escape pod—precious minutes Streithammer did not have.

Do you plan to get me killed, like your last Wizzo? Streithammer's words cut into Deke's mind as if she'd stabbed him with the Ka-Bar.

Deke glanced back, again. Blood dripped off safety harness, seat, and fingers. Dead? He couldn't be sure.

"Panther?" Deke asked. "You still with me?"

A shallow head nod and then a groan. "You don't get a new Wizzo yet, asshole," came the hoarse reply.

A weak smile pushed past the horror and fear on Deke's face. "We got a problem, buddy. We can't trap on the boat, got to eject. It'll take time to pick us up."

Another nod.

Deke sucked in a breath. "You can't wait that long."

"Tough call," Streithammer coughed. "I trust you." She shivered and passed out.

"Panther?' Deke implored, an octave higher. No answer.

"Fifteen, Ramrod." Deke called the boat.

"Go, Ramrod."

"Say ETA for pick up if we eject."

"Standby."

Seconds became years in Deke's mind.

"SAR states thirty minutes, plus," the controller said.

Deke stared at the instruments. Streithammer didn't have five minutes, much less half an hour.

"Request immediate trap." Deke commanded.

We live or die together, Deke thought to Streithammer.

"Roger, you are number one," came the controller's unhurried voice.

Deke entered the approach below the other fighters and bombers stacked in holding patterns above the Lovell. Abeam the carrier he slowed to 300 KPH.

The XSI-58 twitched a warning through Deke's seat—any slower and it would kill him. One last turn pointed Deke at landing bay four's Optical Landing System lights. Deke fought the rebellious interceptor as it closed with the Lovell.

Deke's vision blurred. Still in the cockpit, he also stood next to a grave; the military issue, stone marker bore Jamal's name. A seared hand reached for Deke through the green, Arlington sod. In it, Jamal offered a third alternative: the red pill.

Deke blinked. No longer in the cemetery, Jamal's face had joined him in the cockpit. Deke reached down, tapped the hidden boot heel release, and retrieved the thousand lethal milligrams.

You owe me. Jamal's words echoed in Deke's mind. *You can have peace with me, no more nightmares.*

"Laura will die," Deke reasoned.

She's already dead, boss. You are too—for five months—you just won't accept it.

Deke let forth a long, slow breath. He relaxed for the first time since the accident. Clarity dawned: stark, crystalline, liberating. He accepted death—the ever present acquaintance, now turned old friend.

"Okay, Jammy," Deke whispered. "I know what to do."

Jamal drifted from Deke's consciousness and landing bay four filled the windscreen. The Landing Signals Officer stood in a pressurized, armored cupola next to the bay's cavernous mouth and operated the Optical Landing System to guide Deke' approach. The protective doors slid aside, water vapor sublimated to ice fog as the bay de-pressurized and rushed into space's vacuum.

"Check speed," the LSO's urgent voice beat in Deke's headphones. Deke ignored him and raced forward, too fast for the bay's arresting system to stop the XSI-58.

"Bolter, bolter, bolter!" The LSO commanded Deke to abort the landing.

Deke didn't pull up to go around, instead he pitched the interceptor's nose straight down—hard. He smashed into the shoulder straps, let go the controls, and pulled the eject handle.

The self-contained cockpit pod blew clear from the XSI-58, aimed straight at the landing bay. The fuel laden fuselage careened away from the Lovell, and with it, any potential fire.

Two hundred meters before the landing bay entrance, Deke fired the braking thrusters. The pod shuddered. Deke almost blacked out under the sudden load, and then the pod clanged onto the deck. Sparks flew as it careened toward the far bulkhead. The bay's overhead lights shone rapid, stroboscopic flashes through Deke's canopy and the arresting gear's energy barrier awaited, calibrated for the whole XSI-58, not the small pod.

"Oh shit!" Deke cried, and the world went black.

"The defendant may remain seated," Admiral Dikembe Uto said.

As if I could stand, anyway, Deke thought, and shifted in the wheel chair.

Uto cleared his throat. "This court martial finds Lieutenant j.g. Deke Ulfgier not guilty of all seven counts brought against him."

A murmur arose behind Deke and then faded under Uto's glare.

"This court believes Lieutenant Ulfgier acted with great bravery and initiative under extraordinary circumstances. He is a credit to his unit which won a great, yet costly, victory against the enemy. You are dismissed Lieutenant."

"See, I told you things would work out," Ensign Laura Streithammer whispered in Deke's right ear—the only good one. She swing around in the Navy issue conference chair, grabbed crutches from under the faux-mahogany table, and struggled to her feet. "Doc says a few more weeks and you can scrap the chair, too."

Deke didn't smile. "But they'll never let me fly again."

"You really want back in?"

Deke didn't reply, just stared past Streithammer at the hearing room's door.

"Can't lie to me." She winked.

Deke grasped the quarter century old motorized chair's control stick with his right hand, the left still had stainless steel pins in it, and trundled toward the exit. Streithammer swung alongside on the crutches, left leg in a cast. They passed Commander Jenkins, who refused eye contact with Deke, and then into the fortified space station's corridor.

"Looks like we've both got a lot of spare time on our hands, got any plans?" Streithammer asked, and bit a lower lip.

"Nope."

"Well then, you have a minute for a beer."

"Guess so."

Streithammer put a hand on Deke's shoulder. "Thank you," she said.

Deke nodded. A solitary tear escaped and ran down a cheek.

"Come on, flyboy. I'm buyin'." Streithammer laughed and

launched down the corridor. Deke rammed the control stick forward in pursuit. He rummaged in a pocket, and as he passed a waste disposal port, he tossed the red pill away.

Song's End
By Carol Hightshoe

"If I ever get my hands on Mallory," Selaynia said, ducking behind a support pylon and glancing at her partner. The wolf only bobbed his head as several sudden explosions interrupted the rest of her statement.

:*Only if I don't beat you to him,* Shadowmist said.

Selaynia grinned at the bloodlust she felt from the wolf. Not that she blamed him. Only a month ago, the Confederation agreed to meet with former Alliance Commander Mallory to discuss his terms to convince his group to end their attacks against the Confederation.

It had been almost five years since the Alliance's defeat and surrender. For the majority of the planets that had been claimed by the Confederation, life had gone on as if nothing had changed. And for those planets—nothing had.

The only planets that were still fighting against the Confederation were the planets that had made up the government of the Centauri Alliance. They had all been offered positions within the planetary assembly, but they had refused. So, unlike the other planets, they didn't have a voice within the Confederation's government.

It was a change from the previous set-up. Under the policy of the Centauri Alliance government, each of the member planets were able to have a representative in the congress, but they could only offer opinions; they were not allowed an equal vote.

Most of the member planets hadn't cared. As long as the Alliance was providing them with protection and a forum to voice grievances against other planets, they pretty much carried on as they would have without the Alliance government. Now, with the Confederation, they had been given a voice and most felt that was something worth keeping.

Mallory and his rebels had started out hitting Confederation bases along what had been the border between the Confederation and Centauri Alliance territory, but within the last year as support for his group dropped, they turned to hitting targets on planets that had previously been members of the Centauri Alliance. Now, with the Confederations agreement to meet and discuss a cessation of hostilities, Mallory seized the opportunity to attack the Confederation delegates.

Selaynia, her partner Bobby McKeon, and their wolf partners had been asked to come to the meeting by Shyreth. The Wyvern told her he respected her opinion and knew she would probably be the closest thing to an unbiased observer who could be found and accepted by both groups. She doubted Commander Mallory would agree; the man hadn't trusted her when she showed up on Melpomene station. He could never get past the idea she had defected from the Alliance to the Confederation. With Nolan's death, she really had no way to prove it had been part of an Omega mission. Even with the *testing* he and another telepath had done that showed it was just a well orchestrated deception to infiltrate the Confederation—he had never really believed her. Nothing happened since she left Melpomene station to make her believe he changed his mind.

Another explosion caught her attention; they needed to get out of this part of the station and to the security office. McKeon still had access to the security overrides and wanted to try and get the containment fields up so they could isolate the two groups and at least get a temporary stop to the shooting. Time enough to get anyone not involved off the station and to safety.

"This one," McKeon pointed to a small access panel. "This one leads to the central catwalk. From there, I can get us into the security corridor and to the secondary security office."

Selaynia paused. "Can you activate the overrides from there?"

McKeon nodded. "That's the only place they can be activated. Idea being only the security chief or someone they designated would have access to that area."

*

McKeon stopped and motioned for his wolf partner to lead the way. Smokeshadow nodded, dropped her head a bit to get through the small opening and carefully went in. McKeon followed the wolf and waited for Selaynia to follow him. Shadowmist would follow her.

"There they are," McKeon struggled to turn around in the tight crawlspace. He heard Shadowmist's growl and Selaynia's command to the wolf to stop.

Another explosion rocked the area, the noise deafening in the confined area. McKeon covered his head as debris fell around him, trapping him in the crawlspace. Smokeshadow's howls filled his ears and mind as he heard her scratching and clawing to get to him.

"Selaynia!" There was no answer in the darkness.

McKeon choked on the dust and smoke and he heard Smokeshadow's continued howls. He tried to reach the wolf through their link, but all he could sense was grief and pain. He took another deep breath.

"Selaynia! Shadowmist!" He projected his desperation as he called their names. Slowly, he felt Smokeshadow's mind reach out to his.

:*Shadowmist is dead. I can't sense Selaynia,* she whispered in his mind.

Shadowmist dead? McKeon shivered. He had to get to Selaynia quickly. He might not be Canthralian, but he was bonded to a Canthralian Wolf. He understood the danger to the human partner if the bond was broken like this.

: *We can't go back that way,* Smokeshadow said. : *We need to get to the security office. If Mallory and his people have her, we can locate her after you have them isolated.*

McKeon nodded. He hated the idea of leaving her behind, especially with what she would be suffering, but Smokeshadow was correct, the best way for him to help her was to finish what they started.

*

: *Wait. There's someone moving up ahead.*

McKeon froze as Smokeshadow crept slowly forward. This was taking too long, he needed to get to Selaynia now.

: *We will get to her.* Smokeshadow's tone was harsh and he realized his emotions were wearing on her.

: *Clear.*

McKeon began moving forward again. They had reached the intersection he was looking for. There to his right was an access door. This one had a security panel next to it preventing it from being easily opened.

He wiped his right hand on his pants, it was soaked in sweat, then placed it on the panel. It cycled through a scan and flashed red. Not recognized.

"Please tell me the system hasn't been reset," he whispered wiping his hand again. He held his breath as he waited for the panel to scan his hand a second time. This time, the light flashed green and the door opened. He followed Smokeshadow into the corridor.

McKeon stood up as the door behind him closed. Fortunately, even though you had go through several crawlspaces, the security corridor was a normal hallway. The lights flickered on as they moved quickly to the next door. After the security panel verified his palm print, he had to key in his security code and then wait while another scanner checked his retinal pattern. He held his breath as he waited for the door to open.

McKeon quickly stepped to his right as the door opened and Smokeshadow darted into the room. The lights were voice activated and he waited until the wolf bumped his hand before ordering them on.

The room was just as he left it before the Centauri Alliance abandoned the station. Even the small box of message crystals was still sitting on the console. Messages he had received from Selaynia, when she had been in the Confederation, and passed to Nolan.

"Damn it!" He threw the box across the room.

: *You need to control your emotions. We can't help her until the fighting is contained.* Smokeshadow pressed against him and whined softly.

"Right." He pressed his hand against the console and waited for the system to activate.

"Security Chief McKeon recognized," the computer said. "Please verify security code."

"Security code: zero-delta-theta-four-alpha-mike," McKeon said. The system was keyed to both the code and his voice print.

"Verified." The console finished powering up and he started getting the security shields in place.

*

"Shyreth, please meet me in the security office," McKeon said. "Your nickname for my partner will temporarily lower the shields for you to pass through."

: *You know I hate being called fuzzy.* Smokeshadow said.

"I know, but he is the only one who calls you that and we need him to get this situation under control." McKeon leaned back in his chair and waited. The security corridor connected to the security office so he and Smokeshadow had gone straight there once the fields were up and combatants contained.

"McKeon. Fuzzy." The wyvern stepped into the office and the shield reappeared behind him. "First things first. We were able to get Selaynia to the infirmary before the shields went up."

McKeon looked up at Shyreth. His normally bright red scales were dulled by a layer of dust and his long gold hair was matted and streaked with soot. Wyverns had always reminded him of a little of a dragon, but with features that were almost human. "Shadow?"

Shyreth dropped his head slightly. "I'm sorry. I've asked the doctor to keep her unconscious until you and Smokeshadow can be with her."

McKeon stared at the Wyvern. It was never easy to read them. Their reptilian faces betrayed very little emotion, but the fact Shyreth had not used Smokeshadow's nickname told him more than any facial expression could. He was worried about Selaynia also.

"Do you vouch for those you brought with you?" McKeon asked.

Shyreth nodded.

"Good." McKeon began typing several commands into the computer on his desk. "The fields will recognize the Confederation badges your security people are wearing and allow them to pass. I want you to have them coordinate rounding up Mallory's men and getting them confined. Make sure they also take at least one member of Alliance security, who wasn't involved in Mallory's attack with them."

Shyreth nodded. "I will. Before I start on that, let's get you to the infirmary."

*

McKeon sat quietly as the doctors worked on Selaynia.

:*She needs to go home,* he heard Smokeshadow say. :*She is trapped in her mind and without help, we will not be able to reach her.*

McKeon nodded. "I know, but taking her to Canthralas will not be easy. She is considered an exile. Her clan will not accept her return.

The wolf turned her head slightly and McKeon saw pain in her eyes as well.

:*Not her clan—the wolves. She needs the wolves. I can guide you to Canthralas and help you call the pack. But we need to hurry, the longer she is trapped like this, the harder it will be to bring her back.*

McKeon stood up. "I'll let Shyreth know we're leaving. Stay with her."

*

McKeon glanced over at Selaynia. They had been in the Omega shuttle for three weeks and finally reached Canthralas. During that time, she hadn't spoken a single word. She only ate when he actually put something in her hands, choosing to just sit and stare out the small viewport at the stars.

The doctors at Athena Station Twelve had healed her physical injuries, but she refused to talk to anyone regarding the emotional ones. Smokeshadow was staying close to Selaynia. Through their bond, he could tell she was trying to reach the woman. He only hoped the wolves would be able to bring her out of the grief and despair she was trapped in and give her a reason to live again.

He guided the shuttle through the atmosphere and headed for the mountains; to an area Smokeshadow had shown him in his mind. It was a place where the wolf packs would gather and it was here, she would try to help him call the packs. As far as his wolf partner was knew, no one had called a gathering of the packs for several generations. The only person she was aware might be able to do so was Selaynia who was one of very few humans to have ever been able to hear the wolf song.

Several years ago, Smokeshadow helped create an illusion in which Selaynia called a gathering of the packs in these same mountains. She hoped what she had seen and learned in that experience would allow her to help him to issue the call.

McKeon carefully landed the shuttle in a small valley surrounded by the Mist Peaks. Selaynia let him guide her out of the shuttle and to a spot a few yards away where she could sit against a rock. Her once bright silver-grey eyes were dark and empty as she stared at him, not even acknowledging he was there. McKeon fought the tears he felt burning in his eyes as he looked down at the shell she had become.

Smokeshadow laid down next to Selaynia and placed her head in her lap. McKeon felt a brief surge of hope when Selaynia moved her hand and began stroking the wolf.

Maybe there is a chance we can save her after all, he thought.

:*I need you to focus on our bond,* he heard Smokeshadow whisper in his mind. :*You need to see that bond extending out to all of the wolves on Canthralas. You need to hear the wolf song and let it call to them.*

McKeon nodded and sat down a short distance away from Selaynia and tried to clear his mind of everything except the bond he shared with Smokeshadow. Gradually, he began to filter out his worry over Selaynia, thoughts of those rebuilding on Omega Shadows, and other things that tried to creep in.

He grabbed onto the thread that represented his bond with Smokeshadow and felt it grow stronger. Then, in the distance, he began to hear another wolf singing followed by another and another; until his head was filled with the echoing howls of hundreds of wolves.

:*Good. Now you need to add your voice to the song and ask them to come. Tell them you need their help.*

McKeon nodded, took a deep breath and looked up at the stars as he began to sing. He was shocked for a moment as what he heard coming from his throat was a wolf howl. Long and sorrowful, but in his mind, he heard the words he was singing.

One of the singers has been hurt; she is mind lost and needs your help.

He heard answering howls echoing off the rocks and filling the night. *We come.*

The valley soon filled with hundreds of wolves, all waiting, watching him and Selaynia. He felt Smokeshadow move to stand in front of him almost in a guard position.

:*Who calls the packs?* He heard a deep voice in his mind. :*This is not the one who was touched by wolf song. He is an outsider, not from this world.*

:*He is bonded to me,* Smokeshadow said. :*She who was touched by wolf song is his mate. It is for her that he called the packs.*

:*I am Twilight Shadows.*

McKeon nodded his head to the large grey wolf that stepped past Smokeshadow.

"I am McKeon." He glanced over at Selaynia. "Can you help her?"

:Only if she allows us to. We cannot force her to forget what has happened nor can we force her to talk about it. Your people seem to think forcing someone to relive tragedy and talk about it to others is the only way to help them heal. It is not. What is needed is different for each person. For some, sharing does work, but it cannot be forced.

Twilight Shadows walked over and appeared to be studying Selaynia for several minutes.

:She has lost the song. We must give it back to her. He turned and gave several short barks and yips.

McKeon smiled as several small pups ran out of the crowd of gathered wolves and surrounded Selaynia. He watched as six muzzles pointed toward the sky and they began howling softly, then one of them started whimpering.

Selaynia looked down at the pups and slowly reached out to pet the one that was whimpering.

The pup crawled into her lap, and reached up to lick her face.

:I am called Star Singer," a small voice said as Selaynia cuddled the pup and held him close to her chest.

McKeon smiled. "Thank you," he said to Twilight Shadows. "Now she has a chance."

Star Singer lost his bitch in a rock slide, he was also mind lost— perhaps they will be able to rescue each other. It will take time. She is your mate, don't push her, but don't abandon her, either.

"I won't." McKeon watched as the gathered wolves faded into the shadows and vanished.

"Looks like you have a new friend," he said offering Selaynia his hand.

She nodded as she stood up. She continued to hold the pup tightly and rubbed her face against his.

"Let's go home," he said and gestured toward the shuttle.

Selaynia nodded and followed Smokeshadow.

Still not talking, but at least her eyes aren't dead, anymore, he thought.

He wouldn't push her, she had to work through her grief and pain at her own pace, but he would be there when she needed him.

The pup, Star Singer, glanced at him from over Selaynia's shoulder and grinned.

This story originally appeared in *Tails From the Front Lines*.

Blue Moon
By Francis W. Alexander

"Henri! Commissioner Bratz!" One moment Winston Baker was relaxing in a chair at the helm of a space ship, and the next, lying on the dirt of a strange place. The stone quarry scent betrayed the walls of a cave.

He rose, fully dressed in a helmetless spacesuit, and moved to the place's entrance. The dawn greeted him with a slight breeze tickling his face.

*

As he stepped out of the cave, Winston was welcomed by a yellow sunrise surrounded by cloudless blue skies. Ahead was a rocky plain. The scene reminded him of Mars, except there was nothing but miles and miles of dirt and rock, minus the mountains. He turned and looked at the cave. Resembling a Nazi helmet, it was the tallest structure in sight.

"Is this place a prison?"

To his left and right was the same scene. It reminded him of the rocky way Commissioner Bratz and he had started out. Perhaps the Panel was tying up loose ends by making him disappear, even after he cooperated with them five years ago.

On he walked over the craggy surface.

"Help! Henri?"

The tall light complexioned man looked at the ground for a sign of life. Thankfully, there was enough dust to leave footprints.

He picked up the pace and scanned all around him. Neither mountain nor molehill snatched his attention.

"I've got to be dreaming." He pinched himself. The pain assured him this was real. The scene was as if the New York Philharmonic Orchestra had been transformed into children attempting to perform Tchaikovsky's 1812 Overture after the third day of practice – perfect disharmony. Had someone slipped the spaceship pilot a mickey?

Overhead, the sun curved through the sky faster than normal. Perhaps this planet spun at a speedier rate than earth. The yellow object was now forty-five degrees from the horizon.

Surprisingly, he wasn't hungry. Most of his appetite consisted of wanting to find civilization and weigh anchor. He needed a cliff to leap off, if this loneliness was to be his fate.

A welcome breeze gave him a refreshing smack on the face as he moved in the sweltering heat. With the breeze came voices. He listened intensely. They were definitely the chatter of a woman and some children -- a family.

"Is anyone there?" Winston continued in the direction of the voices directly ahead. Though he couldn't see anybody, the voices seemed to be oh so close.

A fog materialized and surrounded him. This left the man dazed and confused. In the mist, the face of a woman, baby, girl, and teenage boy appeared. They looked familiar, like the picture he had seen of Henri's family members.

Each string of the mist was pieced together and formed a hologram of the four sitting on board a ship. They huddled together as if aiming to form a barrier against a looming threat.

"Henri," the voices said, "why did you leave us, Henri?"

The fog vanished and substituted a grey sky in its place. Irritability and fatigue double-teamed the pilot. His sluggish feet made walking an effort. And it was hot.

The heat squeezed as if aiming to crush him. Winston took off the suit leaving only underwear to make him modest. Knowing that when fatigued, one should exercise, he threw the suit over his shoulder and began to jog.

"Henri!"

His mind and body were definitely not in harmony. All he thought about was Sasha and her family. Had he cheated with her? He doubted it. Maybe he was lying to himself. He had been a pathological liar as a child before his mother took him to a shrink for treatments.

The cave was now a dot on the horizon. Still, he trotted, hoping some kind of hope would materialize.

After jogging for about a mile, he stopped. Around him, nothing but flat plain intersected by horizon. Enough time was wasted. He was heading back. Backtracking memories, he was sure the woman was Sasha. He'd only met the shoulder length haired brunette once and she died five years ago. Was he suffering sensory deprivation? If so, why had he not seen Carol and the kids instead? Not able to answer, he turned back.

As he moved towards the cave, his legs traipsed on as if being held down by lead weights. Hopelessness massaged and tugged on his neck. The temptation to drop to his knees and go no further was strong. Winston's feelings about Henri seemed to take their turn dutch piling the lump of a man that he was. Sasha and the children materialized screaming and crying a couple of feet from him. It looked like an oasis. A burst of fire and smoke consumed them. This was the worst downer ever.

The longer he trudged, the more depression hugged him. Added to his woes was the feeling of schizophrenia, with both downer and anger playing a tug of war with his emotions. He was overwhelmed with the powerful emotion of being sad about Henri's family as if he were the one who had left them behind, clashing with the anger of the Commissioner's deception.

"Be glad your family survived," Bratz had said after Winston confronted him upon hearing about Henri's family. In front of him, they had promised his French friend plenty of seats were available for his friend's people. Then, they convinced Winston to lie and say that an asteroid had destroyed the ship on the way to Earth 2. This deception was done after he found out the Commissioner's loved ones had been given Sasha's seats.

Winston had kept the secret to himself, although he feared that sooner or later, his copilot might find out; especially if they put him in the mnemonizer. If this wasn't the time to be depressed, what was? Then Bratz popped into his mind.

Instead of tumbling further into gloom, the last thought made him angry. He rose and, as if breaking out of steel shackles, moved sternly towards the direction of the cave as the sun stationed itself closer to the horizon. The dome of the cave stood not too far in the distance.

"What would Henri do," he asked. "I'm positive he can help me figure this out. He thought of a song, an almost ancient hit by a singer called Edwin Star.

"Twenty-five miles to you girl..." He sang, placing words where others failed him.

He stopped at the entrance, shocked.

Against the far wall of the cave, was a panel that looked like the cockpit of his ship. To the right was a gurney with white sheeting on top. A steady bleep grabbed his attention.

With furrowed brow, he moved closer to the objects.

After blinking both eyes several times, Winston found himself staring up at a blue ceiling, with the steady beep, beep, beep of a machine nearby. Looking down and to the left, he spotted a silver tube as thick as a water hose running from his arm to a person lying on a gurney beside him.

"Dr. Baker," Carol asked, "are you okay?"

Winston looked up and saw his assistant standing over him.

"I'm still a little groggy," he said, "but everything's coming to me." He rose and looked over at the man lying beside him. Henri would awaken shortly.

Now it was all clear. He, Winston, was the shrink. They needed him and Henri to fly to Ashlon Magnificent to pick up some stranded settlers with time running out, fifteen Parqs to be exact. And the flight path was tricky with only Henri and himself being expert enough to handle the challenge. But his friend was acting strangely. This was the reason the Panel approached him to figure out what the problem was and knock Henri out of his funk.

Winston complied by using the mnemonizer, a machine that would let him enter his copilot's head to experience what Henri felt and sense what the man saw.

"Commissioner Bratz just left," she said. "They'll return in one parq."

"They know I have to analyze, and then find a solution."

"I think they want to be in on the process," she said. "They left an agent. He went to the restroom."

"Aren't two of the Bratz's sons on Ashlon Magnificent?"

"Ashlon Magnificent? No. They are at World Glamourous."

"What?"

"A rebellion has rocked the place and it is imperative that you get his sons and the other ten people out."

"Spoiled brats," Winston said.

You mean," he continued, "they want us to let this settlement of fifty-two people at Ashlon Magnificent perish in the flames of an asteroid, so we can pick up fifteen folks, including their kids from an amusement park?"

She bobbed her head and then moved to take the contraption out of both men's arms and patch them up.

"Can't we do both? Couldn't they find other pilots?"

"For some reason, they only have you two. It would take twelve Parqs to land on either place and clear them out, so you can't do both. The guards are repelling the rebels, and the estimation is that they can hold out for no more than fifteen."

"What is my diagnosis, Doc," Henri said.

"I'm not to be disturbed," Winston said to his assistant. She bandaged his arm, turned, and moved to the exit. He rose and followed her. After she exited, he locked the door. Could he let a settlement die, so the Commissioner's people can live?

"What's the problem," Henri said.

"They want us to go to the Chandelier Hotel at World Glamourous instead of Ashlon Magnificent."

"I heard. What did you find about my problem?"

"Besides," Henri continued, "This might sound cold, but I too would go after my family members first."

Winston sat on the gurney, placed his hands in a v-shape on his lap, sighed, and spoke.

"You are depressed because you still harbor guilt over your family having perished in that crash."

"So I have to take Pschetrixfomin?"

"No."

"Then what?"

"Your family," he said, knowing that sometimes he got his friend out of a funk by angering him, "did not perish in a crash. Bratz substituted some of his family members for your family at the last minute."

"You're lying!"

"Look at the pilot logs for ship A34. That was the last ship to leave

171

Earth 2."

*

"We'll be on time, right?" Bratz stared Winston straight in the eyes after he turned to look at the travelers.

"Yes sir." He smiled and looked at everyone strapped in their seats. If left to Bratz and the Panel, only their loved ones would be rescued from the place. That wasn't right.

"Good." Bratz grinned. The Commissioner seemed to have fallen for Winston's deception.

"Chandelier Hotel at World Glamourous," Henri said. They fired the rockets. The ship rose.

Everyone has some kind of sickness, Winston thought. If he did have a psychological problem, this one felt great.

He sent a message to the settlers:

Everyone be at Port 4A at 06.45.19 EXACTLY!

All the spaceports being alike made this deception easier for him to pull off.

Carefully, the two pilots maneuvered the ship around dangerous asteroids, before plunging into the clouds. On the screen, one couldn't tell one minor planet from the other. Thanks to terraforming, both planets had similar atmospheres.

Moments after the ship docked in port, the Panel and soldiers went over instructions.

"It should take only five centiparqs for us to be back," Bratz said. "I'll leave two soldiers here to guard you."

"Thank you." Winston said.

He gazed at the monitor as the group of fifty-eight moved quickly through Port 5B. When he was sure they were gone, he rose, went to the entrance, and shot the two soldiers standing outside the ship with his napgun. He looked towards Port 4A and spotted figures moving towards the ship.

"Hurry, hurry," he said. "Come and strap yourselves in. We don't have much time."

Once the last settler was in her seat, Winston sat at the helm, closed the doors and fired up the engines.

As the ship climbed, tenseness still held Winston at bay. He turned off the radios so he wouldn't be burdened by guilt at catching the distress calls of the Commissioner and his cronies.

After getting past the exosphere, the pilots made some tricky maneuvers around the dangerous space objects. From that point on, everything was smooth sailing.

A child walked up to Henri and hugged him.

"Thank you, sir," the tyke said. The pilot beamed.

"I couldn't have felt better," Henri said.

"Me neither," Winston replied as the ship headed for Earth 3.

Beyond the Airlock Door
By Terrie Leigh Relf

Raya stared at her face in the small mirror above the sink in her quarters. She had a bit more color in her cheeks, but there were still discolorations beneath her dark brown eyes. Her long red hair was a tangled mess, but she was alive.

Splashing water on her face, Raya changed in a hurry. She didn't want to be late for her appointment with Dr. O'Brian. Fortunately, the psychiatrist's office was just down the hall from her quarters aboard *The Moon Dog,* a state-of-the-art private stellar cruiser.

She walked like she weighed over 200, rather than a mere 107, pounds. It wasn't that Raya didn't trust gravity, as Dr. O'Brian had told her falling, is one of two fears babies are born with, and it wasn't that she didn't trust Ivanovich, the *Moon Dog's* captain, but someone was always yelling or banging around doing maintenance or whatever, and she'd also learned that loud noises was baby-fear number two.

Besides, she was nearly twenty-two, and it was well past time to conquer those fears, learn how to trust others, or more importantly, herself, once again.

"You can get through this, Raya," Dr. O'Brian, the star ship's psychiatrist, told her after their third or fourth session. During the first two sessions, all Raya had done was sob and rock herself. Prior to this, she'd been in the med bay, where Dr. Racini, one of three onboard medical personnel, had kept her under observation, hooked up to an IV to keep her hydrated and nourished. He'd also kept her heavily sedated. Following that, even though she was still afraid to fall asleep, and when she did, would startle awake, she'd begun her sessions with the still-youthful and energetic Dr. O'Brian.

"PTSD is a tricky bugger, but I am here for you now and when you're ready to talk about what you saw. I can teach you some coping strategies, but wouldn't you rather remember without the pain?"

"Of course," she nodded, looking around Dr. O'Brian's office at all the degrees and awards welded into the walls. She liked the older woman with her long silver hair and deep green eyes, eyes that reminded her of wet grass. Would she ever see grass again?

Raya would add being hypnotized as fear number three, as she was afraid what Dr. O'Brian might uncover, what she might be forced to revisit. Ironically, she did so on her own almost daily since the freak accident where she'd lost her older sister and twin, Renata. Renata the smart one, the athletic one, the pretty one. The natural leader. From the time they were toddlers, it was never difficult to tell them apart.

While Raya hadn't known the other team members well, she had liked them. What's more, Renata had liked them, which seemed to compound her grief.

*

The past few months had been stressful and surreal without Renata, but thanks to Dr. O'Brian, she had been released from the practice spacewalks. The entire trip from Earth to Planet X, or Nibiru, would take approximately six months, and they were almost to Neptune.

At first, Capt. Ivanovich had expressed his belief that getting back out there would be the best cure, but Dr. O'Brian insisted it wouldn't be. "Not everyone handles death—or grief—in the same way, and Raya could be a liability," she told the captain. *Liability* was the magic word, it seemed, as death seemed to go hand-in-hand with space travel.

As a condition of being released from the practice walks, Raya needed to agree to Dr. O'Brian hypnotizing her. She expressed her willingness to do any and everything to move past what happened.

And it was working.

Thankfully, she only had an occasional nightmare now. Besides, what would Renata say? Wherever her older sister was, Raya liked to believe Renata watched over her, and wanted her to be proud.

When Raya could finally pass by one of several airlocks contained on *The Moon Dog* without having a meltdown, Dr. O'Brian had her stand by an open airlock. Gradually, she was able to step inside, then eventually *be* inside with the door closed. The hiss still made her adrenalin race, but Dr. O'Brian had a few techniques to give her a nice endorphin release. "Like chocolate, only better," she would say with a knowing wink.

While the true test would be when she was suited up, Dr. O'Brian had assured her that she would be ready when that time arrived. "It's also possible you may not need to take that walk as the shuttle bay has interior access. So do most of the escape pods. But don't you think it's important to be familiar with the process? Just in case?" she asked with a gentle smile.

"Of course," Raya responded, and she *did* believe it was important. Renanta had always conducted extra drills. "Muscle memory, little sis. It's all about muscle memory."

Of course, there was oh-so-much more to it than that, Raya knew.

When Dr. O'Brian had finally told Capt. Ivanovich not to press the issue, it had been like an anodyne to Raya. "She'll be ready when she's ready and not a moment before," Dr. O'Brian informed the captain in her lilting, albeit persuasive, voice. "Besides, as I said before, having Raya panic would not be of benefit to the other personnel. Unless, of course, you want to include that possibility in the drills. . ." Her voice trailed off as she raised an expectant eyebrow at him.

"Fine. Just fine, but keep me in the loop," Capt. Ivanovich replied after a long pause, muttering "headshrinkers," under his breath. Dr. O'Brian pretended not to hear. She preferred to think of herself as a mind expander.

It wasn't that Raya believed she deserved preferential treatment; after all, there were others aboard who battled an array of issues, including the loss of their friends that day, combined with the assorted ailments that tended to accompany space travel.

Long before they approached Nibiru, Raya watched as others stepped outside the airlock for a spacewalk. Almost all personnel needed to do it. *Cross-training* they called it. Once they neared the elusive planet's orbit, *The Moon Dog* would prepare to launch a series of observation satellites. If they received the *all clear*, the shuttles would do flybys, then the first landing teams would be dispersed. No one talked about how long *The Moon Dog* might maintain orbit prior to landing. If they didn't need to scuttle the ship, that is, which was yet another fear that would occasionally stalk Raya.

What ifs continued to plague her thoughts, and one that rose again and again was what if they came all this way for nothing? What if Nibiru was teeming with life and not interested in having visitors? What if the atmosphere was toxic and they would need to live out the remainder of their lives inside protective domes? What if. . .what if. . .what if?!

As part of her therapy homework and training, every night when she hit her bunk, Raya would spend about ten-to-fifteen minutes running through and visualizing the spacewalk protocols. Now that they were within days of approaching Nibiru, it kept her focused, and being focused was a definite positive.

Raya had no clue how far they had traveled, nor how much time had really passed since they left Earth. She had never had a head for math or anything else that demanded an analytical mind. That was one of Renatta's many areas of expertise.

Nevertheless, even though she knew it was about six months, it only felt like a month or two. She had an electronic planner, and would mark the days off in semi-regular fashion based on her sleep cycles. Since *The Moon Dog's* crew operated around the clock, the system seemed to work despite her sense that time was arbitrary.

It felt like just yesterday when Renanta died. A series of yesterdays repeating themselves ad nauseum, intermingled with a few potential tomorrows. It was the present that seemed particularly awkward, though, like a placeholder or way station for the past and future.

*

The Moon Dog was approaching Nibiru's coordinates, and everything indicated that they were nearing geosynchronous orbit. Renata would be so excited, Raya mused, and longed for just one more day with her sister so that they could watch the approach together. The smaller of the two communications satellites had been launched, and hope was high they would receive a response. So far, nothing. The first shuttle launch was scheduled for the morning at 0600.

To say everyone was excited was a major understatement. The first shuttle crew were saddled up and waiting for launch. Raya watched the screen with the rest of the personnel who could be spared from their various duties. Everything would be recorded, and backed up on multiple systems.

"10-9-8-7. . ." The launch commander's voice intoned. All systems were a go, and shuttle one was released, spiraling downward toward Nibiru's nebulous surface. Shuttles two and three soon followed.

Raya focused on the shuttles, imagining her sister in one of them, seeing her nimble fingers rotate dials, pull toggles, flip switches. She sighed, then glanced to the side, seeing her sister in civvies and wearing her classic enigmatic smile. "I'm beyond words, little sister," Renata whispered. "Beyond words. . ."

Raya laughed, prepared to offer a sarcastic comment, then realized Renata wasn't really there. She was just imagining her. Yes, that was it. After all, this had been her sister's lifelong dream since she'd become obsessed with Sumerian lore and had read Zecharia Sitchin and all the other believers. Including the naysayers.

Raya's thoughts drifted until the announcement came in. . ."All three shuttles report no response, friendlies, or otherwise." She could hear people cheering and felt a moment of euphoria. *We're almost there, Renata. Wherever you are, I hope you will be able to see it, too.*

"Stay tuned for visuals," the voice over the com continued. Their eyes wide with excitement and anticipation, everyone waited for the first close-ups of Nibiru, the elusive planet that would now be their home. Renata had believed that this ship was returning home, that she was truly descended from the Annunaki.

Voices raised in confusion. How could it be? Where a planet should have been, there was nothing, nothing at all. But the shuttles had done a fly-by. . . How was this possible?

And where were the shuttles now? They should have reported in by now. . .

*

To say morale was at an all-time low was an understatement of the highest magnitude. And yet, there was an air of hope aboard *The Moon Dog,* as they were definitely locked into some type of magnetic pull that indicated a planetary orbit. Nibiru, if it was really there, was shrouded in what a few jokingly referred to as a cloaking device. It made sense. After all, weren't the Annunaki a superior race of beings? Given how many thousands of years it had been since their last trip to Earth, their tech would have advanced.

Raya heard a few people talking about taking a leap of faith, calculating the distance to Nibiru's surface, determining a place to land. It just had to be there. The shuttle pilots must have landed, or been pulled in by some sort of docking mechanism. What no one wanted to say was that they had been shot down. Or worse. Raya was sure there could be a worse, although she didn't want to go there.

Capt. Ivanovich and his advisors, including Dr. O'Brian, had been closeted for hours. Raya imagined them discussing contingency plans. If Nibiru really wasn't there, then they would need to find an alternate planet. But which one? No one wanted to return to Earth—or did they? The Trans-National Lunar bases were a possibility, she supposed, remembering that was Renata's Plan B if she didn't make the cut for the Nibiru project.

The stars were incredibly bright, and Raya wondered what the Annunaki called their constellations. Neptune loomed. This, she supposed, was one of the best things about space travel. . .the occasional peace and quiet, the exquisite view from her quarters. Something moved out of the corner of her eye, drawing her attention. Then Renata's voice in her mind, Renata's finger pointing to just beyond Neptune. *Remember that old translation argument I used to go on about?*

Raya nodded as if Renata were actually speaking to her. *Go on.*

Think about it, little sis. Gateway. Doesn't it make you think of portals? Maybe Nibiru isn't really a planet after all, but a portal to other worlds.

If that's true. . .

Exactly. You need to talk to the captain. Convince him. Or better yet, Dr. O'Brian. Talk to her. You can't just hang out here in space forever.

The last comment made Raya chuckle. Then it dawned on her. Renata was really here. Or her spirit was. If anyone would be looking for creative solutions to their dilemma, it was Renata.

*

Raya waited outside Dr. O'Brian's office. Capt. Ivanovich's voice was raised, incredulous. "So you're telling me that Raya claims to be talking to her dead sister and that said dead sister claims Nibiru is a portal, not a planet? That we should just believe her and go full-throttle?"

"That's about it," Dr. O'Brian responded, her voice calm,

reassuring.

"So, I should take the word of a delusional nutcase?"

"Remember what I told you about the special bond between twins? Is it really so far-fetched that Renata would be communicating with her? Or, communication with the dead aside, that there is more to Raya than meets the eye, that perhaps she has a sense of things, remembered something her sister said that while never proved, has never been disproved. . ."

There were several moments of silence, and Raya moved closer to the anteroom door, hoping to hear their murmured comments. She heard footsteps, muffled by the thick cushioned carpet. She moved back to her seat just as the door opened. Dr. Ivanovich glanced at her, his face twisted up in a scowl, then pressed the release for the outside door, stepped through.

"You can come back in, Raya," Dr. O'Brian called.

She sat down on the edge of the pod-like couch, looked up and into Dr. O'Brian's luminous green eyes.

"No doubt you heard all that. I apologize for his inconsiderate language. While it's no excuse, stress is a factor. Regardless of his perceptions, he is actually willing to entertain the possibility."

"So, what now?"

"We wait. See what he decides." Dr. O'Brian looked out her window, her gaze thoughtful. "What an adventure this has been. . ." her voice trailed off, and for the first time, Raya wondered what lead her doctor to join the team.

"Yes, it certainly has been," Raya said.

Dr. O'Brian turned toward her, pursing full lips. "Are you prepared to volunteer?"

"Volunteer for what?"

"To test your theory. Your sister's theory."

"I don't know what you mean. I thought the whole ship. . ." Her eyes widened when she saw Dr. O'Brian's expression, the shake of her head. "But how would I report back? The shuttles weren't able to."

"Apparently, the telemetry may have been malfunctioning. It could be that it was jammed by our friends on Nibiru, either intentionally or as a security measure. Capt. Ivanovich is willing to have a few volunteers go down in the escape pods. Since you posed the possibility that Nibiru is a waystation or portal. . .The fact that we can't see it might mean that the portal is open. I recommended that you go."

"What? You've got to be kidding. No, of course you're not. I. . .I. . .
."

Raya leaned back in the pod couch, pulled up her knees. She felt the faintest touch on her leg, turned to see Renata sitting next to her. *Do it, little sister. I'll be with you.*

"When do I leave?"

"That's the spirit!" Dr. O'Brian got up from her chair and pressed the com to the Captain's office. His assistant delivered the message.

*

"This is crazy," Raya mumbled to herself, tugging the tether, connecting her for a few more moments to *The Moon Dog*, to artificial gravity, to one last day if not on board, at least alive. The tether felt strong enough to reel her in if need be, so she wouldn't be left dangling off the launch pad. Of course, the escape pods had to be attached externally to the ship.

The airlock door slid open and she unclenched her eyes, reached for, grabbed the doorjamb as the silent stare of space sent adrenalin coursing through her. It felt like insects crawling in her brain. Insects burrowing in her skin. She breathed slowly in-and-out, focusing on the exhale, like Dr. O'Brian taught her. In less than a minute, she stopped shuddering.

She wouldn't look down, couldn't look down, but at least her suit's life-support systems were pulsing green. The voice in her com was patient, soothing. While it wasn't Dr. O'Brian, it could have been; the launch commander had a friendly voice.

She clenched her eyes, leaned forward slightly. "Don't leap or dive," the LC reminded her, refraining from saying that that would catapult her too far. She almost laughed as an image of wind whipping through her long red hair filled her mind, but the helmet prevented that, and besides, they were well above those elements.

Why did I ever sign up for this? she sighed, remembering what Renata had said to persuade her. "It's a one-way trip for me, little sister. I can't imagine not having you with me," followed by a smile and a hug.

Oh how Raya missed her sister. Had Renanta known she was going to die? She always assumed that comment meant she planned to live out her natural life on Nibiru.

The interior airlock door hissed close, and Raya barely startled, but she could still feel the adrenalin pumping, her breath slightly ragged until the LC's friendly voice returned, talking her through another system check. There would be a short waiting period before the outer door hissed upon, and she basked in the silence, the irony not lost on her. Then the LC guided her toward the grips, the escape pod just a few meters ahead. Each step felt like her feet were embedded in clay tablets, but she made progress. A few more steps. . .just a few more steps and she would be safe inside the escape pod with the others. A few more steps and her sister's dream of landing on Nibiru would be real. A few more steps and. . .

The pod door glimmered with wan light as she was pulled inside by Dr. O'Brian and Franco, one of the techs. She was shocked to see Dr. O'Brian. "What are you doing here?" She cried out, to which Dr. O'Brian replied, "As I said before, the experience of a lifetime. . ." with a smile. There were others inside, a combination of essential and non-essential personnel. Raya strapped in, closed her eyes as the automatic systems prepared to launch the pod. She closed her eyes, imagined a field of lush green grass, palm trees, the cool sensation of rippling river water, the scent of cinnamon and exotic flowers, golden rooves glittering in the sun.

And then the pod was released and she clung to that image, superimposed upon it, her sister beckoning, as they plummeted to the planet below.

Check out all of the Nomadic Delirium Press titles at:
http://nomadicdeliriumpress.com/blog/shop

Feel free to visit our blog and share your opinions about the stories and poems in this issue. You can also keep up on future Nomadic Delirium Press releases:
http://nomadicdelirium.wordpress.com/

If you've liked what you've read, please become a patron for Nomadic Delirium Press at
https://www.patreon.com/nomadicdeliriumpress